Leaving Sanctuary Behind

Written By Erik Augustine

Leaving Sanctuary Behind
A "romance-thriller" novella written by Erik Augustine

Leaving Sanctuary Behind

Written By Erik Augustine

Author's note: I dedicate this book to my mother, Julie, grandmother, Marietta, & late grandfather, John. You all were a huge inspiration.

And a very special thanks to Laurie, I couldn't have done it without your gratitude and immense help.

Table Of Contents

The Exposition

The year is 1994.

Twenty years have passed since the catastrophic end of World War III, the events of which left a vast majority of the North American nation covered in a thick layer of the toxic weaponized gas known as Ultra-18.

One of the last remnants left of humanity is those citizens who chose to live within Cherry Blossom, a town in rural Pennsylvania encased under a series of interconnected Domes before the bombs fell and the subsequent societal collapse that beheld.

Five Domes made up Cherry Blossom and each served a specific purpose.

Homelands Dome: Tract housing built to shelter the citizens.
Power Plant Dome: A series of Organic Fuel Engines (OFE) that supplied power to Cherry Blossom.
Farmlands Dome: A collection of farms to produce fuel and food for Cherry Blossom.
Overbrook Hills Dome: The town center containing various shops, businesses, factories and government buildings.
Sanctuary Park Dome: A park and nature preserve.

Also including
The Central Hub: A junction that connects all Portway rail tracks to one central location.

The Portway: A tram system connected through various clear tubing tunnels, allowing transportation from Dome to Central Hub and vice versa.

Every Dome was equipped with an Air Recycling System (ARS) containing both a Heating/Ventilation/Air Conditioning System (HVACS) unit and a Dome Meltdown Alarm (DMA) to regulate the temperature and air quality within. Each Dome also included Quick Acting Air Tight Doors (QAATD), Leak Containment Devices (LCD), and Emergency Gas Outbreak (EGO) gas masks as precautionary measures taken to ensure the air within Cherry Blossom was always safe and breathable.

As 1993 came to an end, upon completion of the 2-year term at Career Aptitude School, the graduating class of '93 would be acquiring their new careers within Cherry Blossom. On the first day of the new year, every graduate must report to the Career Office inside the Overbrook Hills Dome to receive their new permanent career.

Seven hundred eighty-two citizens lived within these Dome walls, but 782 would soon begin to decrease.

Chapter 1

The Descent Into Darkness

January 2nd, 1994
2:13 AM
782 citizens exist

A sewer grate arose out of its socket. Two small hands pushed against the dense metal and slid the grate gently across the bright white tile that made up the floor to the Central Hub. From within the sewer tunnel, a figure emerged into the light.

This was Janine Crane. A shorter-than-normal red-headed girl, 20 years old, always known to be boasting a bright and courageous outward attitude. She was one of the three leaders of The Tunnel Society, loved exploring the unknown, and had a sweet innocence about her, acting as a well-disguised camouflage for her involvement in such exploration schemes. On this day, she wore a cream-colored sweatshirt, loose high-waisted jeans, and persistently dirty all-white sneakers.

The Tunnel Society was a secret group formed by the teenagers of Cherry Blossom years prior, with the sole intention of digging a way out and escaping the Dome walls.

Once Janine exited the sewer, she removed the EGO gas mask from her face, clipped it inside her belt loop along with her gardener's shovel, and gently returned the sewer grate to its original position within the floor. She began her walk across the Central Hub toward the Homelands Portway door, built within a wide semicircle aligned with the other Portway doors and took slow steps as she was drowning in exhaustion.

Janine removed the LCD strapped to her back and returned it to its bracket secured to one of two tiled planters, built mirroring each other in the center of the Central Hub, as she trotted past it.

From her visit to the secret tunnels, Janine discovered a Tunneler had successfully broken the barrier to the outer world, but no Tunnel Society members had notified her about such an accomplishment. Before she left the secret tunnels, Janine had walled off the gas-filled corridors the Tunneler left behind with a thick layer of the quick-hardening foam from the LCD. She was now on her way to speak with the first member of the society she could find.

On her journey toward the Homelands Portway door, a noise broke through the silence in the air, causing her to halt in place, stricken with fear.

The movement of the sewer grate, located in the center of the Central Hub, once again lifting out of its snug cutout and sliding coarsely across the floor, filled the room with a horrid sound of scraping metal.

Janine slowly oscillated around and witnessed from within the open sewer tunnel two hands outstretched from the darkness and gripped onto the lip of the hole, pulling against it to lift themselves out.

From the depths of the sewer surfaced a figure Janine had recognized to be Charles Ivory.

Charles Ivory was 64 years old, a bit overweight, and had a long, disheveled gray horseshoe-style mustache. He was always seen wearing his rarely-washed work uniform, topped with his signature white cowboy hat that covered his severely balding scalp. Charles was a war-torn man who had been ravaged by life's cruel intentions, hiding from its wrath behind a bottle. Wrinkles had started to take grasp over his skin and reflected the absence of a life that had been long drained away. He was now a sloshed, ill-mannered husk of his former self and considered by all to be the craziest citizen to live within Cherry Blossom.

Charles pushed himself out of the sewer, lifted his leg, and planted his foot on the tiled floor of the Central Hub. He forced the rest of his body into the open and fully emerged out of the sewers. His face lacked any emotion.

"Hi ... Charles. What were you doing in the sewers? ..." Janine asked nervously, trying to diffuse the thick tension that submerged the pair.

Initially, Janine's fear originated from the idea that her secret involvement in The Tunnel Society had been discovered. She soon realized by Charles' demeanor that this was a different encounter entirely.

Charles did not respond to Janine.

He slowly began to step toward her.

"Charles, what are you doing?" Janine asked, trembling in fear as she slowly stepped backward.

Janine glanced over to the bright red Peace Officer Emergency Call Box located on the wall adjacent to her. She noticed her only means of alerting safety was too far away and most likely unreachable but chose to run for it anyway.

Without hesitation, Janine immediately sprinted toward the Call Box, desperate to save herself.

Charles sprinted after her. Once he was within reach, he swung his arm behind his body and drove it forward into the back of Janine's head. The force of the punch sent her to the ground. She fell to the floor and broke her fall with her hands outstretched in front of her. She lay sprawled out on the tile, writhing in the intense pain that coursed through her body.

Janine turned over onto her back to face her perpetrator. She lay there weak and immobile as she watched Charles step over, leering down upon her akin to a predator over its prey.

Charles, with not an ounce of remorse nor even a resemblance of emotion taking over his face, once again swung his arm back and drove it forward into Janine's face, effectively breaking her nose and knocking her unconscious. Two streaks of blood leaked out of her nostrils, down her face, and dripped to stain the clean white tile with a few droplets of human paint.

Charles turned around, leaned over, and grasped tightly onto Janine's ankle. He then stood up and stepped toward the open sewer tunnel, dragging her body across the ground as he marched closer to his escape. Once he was at the opening, Charles lowered his body down into the sewer, dragging Janine's limp corpse along with. He pulled her body violently into the sewer, accompanied by the sound of heavy flesh being whipped into metal piping by gravity.

Charles pulled his meal deeper into the dark depths below before returning to the top of the pipe, replacing the sewer grate into its original housing within the floor and slithering back into the darkness.

Silence flooded back into the Central Hub as Charles descended deeper into the sewers with Janine's body. The Central Hub was now deafeningly quiet as if nothing had happened. All that was left of the horrific event were the remnants of Janine's blood on a singular tile amongst the hundreds that made up the floor.

Acquiring the taste of flesh commenced a horrific chain of events.

Chapter 2

The Acquisition

January 1st, 1994
7:14 AM
782 citizens exist

Henry Greene was 20 years old, a loner, and a bit of a sarcastic asshole. He was a tall, scrawny guy, had a relatively decent face, and possessed a drained emptiness stained over his aura in neglect of happiness or purpose brought on by the pain of his father's death during the war. Henry was always seen wearing a dark brown canvas jacket, a shirt tucked into pale blue jeans cuffed at the ankle, and dirty monochrome high-top sneakers. He was convinced life itself was against him, destined to cause him turmoil as a cruel joke. At this point, he accepted the predicament he was born into and was unhappily used to it, being in on the joke himself.

Overall, he was average. Just another one of the 782.

Henry stood in line, suffocated by the smoke stained pastel sage of the soulless Career Office walls, feeling anxious. As the young woman standing in front of him fell out of line, he stepped forward and was now face-to-face with the Career Machine.

The Career Machine was a large device, built longer than it was wide, that took up a substantial part of the Career Office. The front of the machine was a tall, slender operational mechanism that fed into the larger back end of the device. The machine itself was painted a dark forest green with pearly white accents.

A small plaque was attached to the face of the device, toward the top, reading "Career Machine" with smaller text underneath displaying "*Enjoy making a living!*"

Henry nervously stared at the words as he reached into his back pocket and pulled out his Citizen Card. He inserted the card into a thin slot within the machine until it stuck out halfway. He then reached over and pushed a small white button on the face of the device, causing the Citizen Card to be taken and swallowed into the machine by its internal mechanisms. After three seconds, a palm-sized manila envelope was ejected from the same slot, accompanied by a high-pitched ding.

Henry took the small envelope out of the machine and proceeded to fall out of line, quickly exiting the Career Office. He stood outside within the Overbrook Hills Dome, drowning in anxiety and anticipation. He stared down at the envelope in his hands, almost too scared to open it.

Henry inhaled sharply and exhaled slowly before slipping his thumb and index finger inside the envelope. He gripped onto his new Citizen Card and could feel the warmth of the fresh ink against his fingertips. He slid his new Citizen Card out, letting the envelope fall to the ground in yearly tradition, and stared at the recently printed text.

Henry's face slowly shifted from being nervous to being appalled as he read the career he was chosen for.

"*Sanctuary Park Overnight Groundskeeper.*"

The words stared back with horrific implications.

Fully processing what this meant, He squeezed his Citizen Card out of anger, almost snapping it. He began to shake the card in a pantomime strangulation, trying to inflict his anger onto it.

"Fuck!" Henry said through his gritted teeth in rage.

Henry's outburst caused a few bystanders to become onlookers. Noticing he was almost drawing a crowd, He relaxed and kept his composure. He then released his grip and turned over his Citizen Card to see if there was anything else printed on the back.

At the bottom of the card, in small print, it read:
"All careers are final."

Henry internalized his pain with a deep sigh. He returned his Citizen Card to his back pocket once again and proceeded to retrieve a pack of cigarettes and a lighter from his jacket pockets. He put a cigarette in his mouth and lifted the lighter up, sparking the end. Henry returned everything to his jacket and began his journey toward the Sanctuary Dome as he tried to smoke his problems away.

7:48 AM

Once arriving at the Sanctuary Dome Henry sat patiently in the Portway Kart as it made itself flush with the Sanctuary Dome Portway door. Once the Kart settled, he reached up and pressed a button labeled "open/close door" on the Portway Kart's control panel. He was then greeted with loud metallic booms that echoed throughout the Kart.

Henry could hear a muffled buzzer ring out from the other side of the Portway door before it unlocked and slowly swung open by itself. He stood up off the Kart seats and stepped over toward the

Portway Kart door before unlocking it and sliding the door along its rails inside the Kart wall.

The thick smell of nature met Henry's nose as he stepped out of the Portway Kart and onto fresh grass. He took a couple of steps forward before looking up and seeing a deformed and corroded black gate archway with the name "Sanctuary" displayed in metal letters.

The Portway door slowly shut itself closed behind Henry, automatically locking once an airtight seal was established.

Henry returned his gaze down from the archway and saw a dirt trail displayed out in front of him. He followed the trail for a while until, through the trees, he could see a building in the distance.

Henry cut through the trees that surrounded him and walked straight toward the structure. He took a final step forward and was now standing, hidden by the shadows of the trees above, observing the face of the building.

The front of the building was made up of glass panels with a single glass door in the center. The rest of the surrounding structure was built out of brick that had been painted white with a thin green line that wrapped around the entire exterior. The inside of the building was a remnant of the past, originally built in the late '60s, resembling that of a camping lodge.

Inside the building, Henry could see a man sitting at a desk on the left side of the room, reading a book, facing toward the door.

This man was Charles Ivory.

This was the reason why Henry didn't want to work for Sanctuary. Charles was infamous within Cherry Blossom, but not for any good reason. Not much was known about him, but a lot was said about him. Out of all the rumors, the only things Henry knew to be true were that Charles was a veteran of World War III, he was known to make up wild stories, and he was a raging alcoholic.

Everyone in Cherry Blossom was put in an unsettling disgust by Charles, almost fearing him. No other citizen ever spoke to him or even looked in his general direction. Until now.

Henry hung his head and exhaled a deep sigh before walking toward the front door of the building. Once he was at the door, he pushed against the metal handle and let himself in.

Henry stepped inside and stood next to the entrance, staring at Charles as he let the door shut behind him. He was unable to think of what to say.

Charles lifted his head from the book he was reading and stared antagonistically at Henry. He could feel Charles' eyes pierce his soul. Charles slapped his book closed with an audible soft boom, letting it rest atop the desk, and sat up in his chair, smiling deviously at Henry.

"Take a seat," Charles said with a grin as he spoke in his native southern draw.

Henry noticed medical tape wrapped and surrounded bloody gauze on Charles' right hand as he motioned toward a pair of chairs sitting in front of the desk.

Henry stepped toward the chairs. He pulled on the back of one to offer room for himself to sit. Henry then lowered himself down slowly into the seat.

"What happened to your hand?" Henry asked curiously.

"Oh, that? Damn little rabbit bit me the other day," Charles explained.

"How'd that happen?" Henry asked, further inquiring.

"I was trying to catch him, obviously … unfortunately, that lil' bastard got away again! If you see a gray rabbit with blue eyes, let me know," Charles said

"Why you tryin' to catch him? Is it munchin' on your plentiful harvest?" Henry asked with a spitefully sarcastic southern twang, mocking Charles' own accent.

"More like on the other rodents, but hey! That's not important right now …" Charles said, throwing out the questioning as he began to study Henry.

Henry knew of a common rumor spread around Cherry Blossom stating Charles was, in fact, himself eating the small rodents inside Sanctuary Park. Knowing this and hearing Charles' statement about the matter Henry assumed he was lying, trying to cover his tracks.

Henry and Charles stared at each other for a moment. Henry felt an awkward tension fill the room before being displaced by a single question.

"So … you're my new Overnight Groundskeeper, huh?" Charles asked smugly as he sat back in his chair, folding his arms.

"I guess so …" Henry said, matching Charles' smugness in tone.

"Alrighty then! Let's get started," Charles said enthusiastically.

"Wait! Aren't you going to see if anyone else shows up?" Henry asked, confused.

"Not that many people get selected for this position … eh, one or two at the most, if that. When I started, it was just me and the head Groundskeeper. Yep, consider yourself lucky, son; this job doesn't get picked every year. It's seen as sort of a rarity in the system," Charles explained.

"Good to know …" Henry said, trying to hide how upset he was inside with sarcasm.

"Yep, looks like it's just going to be you and m-" Charles tried to say before being interrupted.

The front door of the building had opened once again. Henry and Charles both adjusted their attention toward the interruption.

Standing in the entranceway of the room was a girl. Henry immediately recognized her.

This was Ruby Jenkins.

Ruby was 21 years old, known to dress gothic, and considered to be a strange girl. She was quite pretty, having shoulder-length, deep black curly hair and a beautiful, distinct array of freckles across her nose and cheeks. She wore tortoiseshell glasses that were held together with electrical tape, a deep black zip-up hoodie covering a band T-shirt from the "old world," jet black heavily ripped jeans overtop fishnets seen through the torn denim, and bright red high-top sneakers. She was always vivacious, rarely seen upset or discouraged, hiding her internal struggle to be more opportunistic behind her playful exterior.

When Henry saw Ruby, he felt as if life was toying with him.

Ruby removed a pair of headphones from her head and hung them around her neck. She hit pause on the cassette player clipped to her belt and stepped farther into the room toward Henry and Charles.

"What can I help you with, young lady?" Charles asked Ruby.

Ruby retrieved her new Citizen Card from her pocket, holding it up, as she gave a smirk and tilted her head toward it.

"Here for my job!" Ruby said with a playful attitude.

"Well, come on over and have a seat. I was just about to get started," Charles said as he motioned toward the seat next to Henry.

Henry had always liked Ruby ever since he saw her for the first time, several years earlier. Although he felt it was a feeble fever dream to think she would feel the same, Henry had now been given the worst punishment and the greatest gift all in the same day. Now, for the rest of his working life, Henry would be alongside the craziest man he knew and the girl of his dreams.

Ruby returned the card to her pocket before she walked over to the chair next to Henry and pulled on the backrest to offer herself room to sit. Ruby then sat down and crossed her legs over one another.

"Alrighty then! Now, that should be everybody," Charles said.

Henry stared down at his shoes as he laid back and processed everything that was happening at this moment. Henry then slowly glanced over at Ruby, making sure this was actually happening before his very eyes.

Ruby saw Henry's movement in her peripheral vision and glanced back over at him. The pair made eye contact that held for eternal seconds in their minds before their attention was diverted back to Charles once he spoke.

"Well, as you two should already know, this is an overnight position. Work starts at 10 pm and ends at 7 am. I'll be keeping track of your hours, so be sure to use your radios to clock in and out. No need to worry about it right now, though; I'll have both of your gear ready for you later tonight. What size do you want your uniforms?" Charles informed the pair before asking.

"Large should be good," Henry plainly stated.

"Medium will do," Ruby answered.

"Got it. The only thing to really do now is to give you both a tour of the park. What do ya say?" Charles propositioned.

The pair looked at each other once again, seeking assurance, then back toward Charles.

"Okay!" Ruby said with excitement.

"Alright," Henry said in reluctant acceptance.

"Great!" Charles said once he heard their responses.

Charles pushed his chair away from the desk and stood up. He began to grunt slightly as he adjusted his belt around his fat gut.

"I'll get my coat on. You two go ahead and wait for me out in the red truck on the side of the building here," Charles said as he pointed toward the wall.

Henry and Ruby simultaneously stood up. Henry walked in front of Ruby as the pair made their way to the front door.

Once at the door, Henry reached forward, pulled against the handle, and held it open. He stepped out of the way and motioned for Ruby to go ahead in front of him. Ruby appreciated his kind gesture and stepped through the doorway into the outdoors. Henry followed Ruby as he, too, ventured outside.

Henry and Ruby walked along the glass panels until they reached the edge of the building. Once rounding the corner of the structure, both were confronted by an old red rusty pickup truck parked out in the grass.

"Shotgun!" Ruby said excitedly to claim ownership of the passenger seat.

"Shit!" Henry said with playful anger.

"Ya snooze, ya lose!" Ruby teased as she walked over toward the passenger side door of the truck.

Ruby opened the passenger door and climbed inside, closing it once she sat comfortably in the seat. Henry walked toward the back side of the vehicle, lifted himself over the frame, and climbed into the bed of the truck. He sat with his back against the rear window and looked out into the forest.

Henry gazed at the abundance of foliage that surrounded him. As he took in the forest he noticed something move off in the distance. Henry squinted his eyes and leaned forward to get a better look. As his eyes adjusted their focus to the movement afar, all he saw was the blurred figure of a deer disappearing into a patch of shrubbery. Henry knew Sanctuary had its own ecosystem of animals and tried to become comfortable with the fact that this Dome would now be a significant part of this new stage in his life.

A few minutes passed before Charles finally came outside and rounded the corner of the building. He walked around the front of the truck and proceeded to get into the driver's side of the vehicle, rocking it slightly as he sat his heavy figure inside. Charles shut the driver's door forcibly behind himself and pulled out a ring of keys from his jacket pocket, inspecting them until he found the correct one. He inserted the key into the ignition and started the engine. Charles put the truck in reverse and pulled away from the building; he then shifted the gears into drive and drove the truck forward along a wide open path created as a trail that serpentined throughout the forest.

The trio immersed farther into Sanctuary Park.

Charles had now begun the tour.

"That building we just left was Station 1; That's my office. Right now, we're on our way to Station 2," Charles said as he drove at a slow, steady pace through the reserve.

After a short journey through the forest, the trio drove up toward another building. Ruby could see Station 2 through the windshield as they approached. Moments later, Charles stopped the truck on its path a short distance outside the Station with the vehicle's driver side facing toward the building. Henry and Ruby both turned and observed the structure.

"That right there is Station 2. Henry, this is where you will be every night," Charles explained.

Henry looked on from the bed of the truck and studied Station 2. It was identical to Station 1.

Charles slowly drove away and continued the tour, eventually arriving at the back side of the Dome. He stopped the truck along its path, 80 meters away from a small mausoleum built in lonesome recluse in the back of Sanctuary Park.

Charles pointed out his driver-side window at the mausoleum in the distance.

"That there is the Crypt. You two are probably too young to have been inside yet, but that's where we in Cherry Blossom house the deceased. It's basically a spiral stairwell of coffins stored in the walls. Creepy as shit if you ask me," Charles explained.

The pair studied the mausoleum in all of its chilling sadness. Charles then drove away from the Crypt and across Sanctuary Park toward another building.

Charles halted the truck in front of the final identical Station.

"This here is Station 3, and of course, this will be your spot, Ruby," Charles said.

Henry and Ruby studied the building for a moment before Charles eventually drove away.

Charles continued the tour and drove around Station 3 past the back side of the building.

A large machine was built a short distance from Station 3, sitting in the grass, pressed against the Sanctuary Dome wall. Protruding out from the side of the machine was a clear tube that attached to the Dome wall and fed from the outer world.

Charles parked the vehicle adjacent to the machine and cut off the engine. He exited the truck and walked over toward the face of the device. Henry and Ruby watched as Charles left them behind, and they soon followed.

"This right here is Sanctuary's ARS. Part of the job will be each of us taking turns replacing the filter to this thing about once a month. The three lights on top will indicate if we need to replace the filter or if the machine is broken. When they're solid green, that's normal; if they're flashing yellow, the filter needs to be changed; if they're flashing red and you hear the DMA siren, you better run for the door," Charles said as he pointed at the three large bulbs sticking out of the top of the machine.

Charles walked closer toward the ARS.

Within the face of the machine was a large metal tube, built with a window showing the level of its purple-frothing slime-filled contents, that sat snugly inside the ARS. Charles reached forward and gripped onto a handle attached to the tube. He yanked on the handle until the filter was released from the machine. Once the filter had exited the ARS, the lights atop the machine began to flash yellow.

Charles walked over to Henry and shoved the ARS filter into his chest.

"Go ahead and fix it," Charles said, sternly smug.

Henry instinctively grabbed onto the filter, holding it in both arms, as Charles let go. He reached over the metal tube with one hand and gripped the filter by the handle, resting it by his side as he walked over toward the face of the ARS. Henry lifted the tube up and shoved it back into the open slot within the machine, just as it was before. The lights on top of the ARS switched from flashing yellow back to solid green.

"Aye, look at that. You're a natural!" Charles said.

Ruby smiled at Henry.

"Alright. When the time comes, extra filters can be found in your Station's back room. If you ever need more, I'll have to place an order, so just let me know ahead of time. The sprinkler system kicks on from 3 am to 4 am, so if you like to keep dry, I'd recommend staying in the Stations around then. Besides that, that's pretty much the whole park; any questions?" Charles asked.

Henry and Ruby both shook their heads in denial.

"You guys need a lift back to the Portway door?" Charles asked.

"Yeah, that'd be great," Ruby answered for the both of them.

Henry turned to look at Ruby.

"Shotgun!" Henry shouted.

"Dammit!" Ruby said as she laughed.

"Alrighty then, let's head out!" Charles said.

The trio then proceeded to get back into the vehicle. This time, Henry was in the passenger seat and Ruby sat in the bed of the truck.

9:02 AM

Charles drove Henry and Ruby back across Sanctuary to the Portway door, stopping the truck in front of the Sanctuary archway with the vehicle's passenger side facing toward the Portway door. Henry and Ruby exited the vehicle and stood next to each other as they both looked back into the passenger window at Charles.

"I'll see you both tonight at 10 o'clock. Got it?" Charles asked sternly.

"Got it!" Henry and Ruby answered in unison.

Charles then began to drive away from the pair and back toward Station 1. Henry and Ruby both turned around and walked toward the Portway door.

"Hey, I almost forgot something ..." Henry said.

"Oh yeah? What's that?" Ruby asked, a little confused.

"Jinx, you owe me a soda!" Henry said, very proud of himself.

"You son of a bitch," Ruby said as she smiled and pushed Henry.

"Hey, don't hate the player, hate the game," Henry teased as he shrugged his shoulders.

Henry and Ruby were now standing in front of the Portway door. Henry walked over to a thin metal pole sticking out of the dirt. Atop the pole at waist height was a metal box with a button labeled "Call Kart."

Once he pressed the button, the sound of a bell ringing emitted from a speaker built within the Portway door's frame. Henry rejoined Ruby as they waited for the Kart to arrive.

"So ... what's your whole read on Mr. Ivory?" Ruby asked.

"Oh, you mean cuckoo Charles? ... I don't really know, he seems alright, but we only spent, like, an hour with him," Henry answered.

"Hmm ... yeah, I just heard a lot of stories, I guess ..." Ruby said.

"Yeah, I heard he eats the rodents in the park," Henry said, trying to relate.

"I've heard that one ..." Ruby laughed.

Ruby paused for a moment.

"... I heard that he lives out here in Sanctuary. Doesn't ever return to the Homelands," Ruby said.

"That's why he smells so bad!" Henry said in sarcastic surprise.

Ruby giggled at Henry's comment before he too, joined in and they laughed together.

The Portway Kart arrived at the Sanctuary Dome, and a loud buzzer rang out from the speaker.

Henry stepped toward the Portway door. He gripped and twisted the big hatch wheel on the face of the door to unlock it. Once fully rotated, Henry pulled against the hatch wheel and walked the door along its hinges until there was enough room to step through.

"After you," Henry said

"Thanks!" Ruby said.

Ruby stepped forward and grasped the latch to the Portway Kart door. Ruby unlocked it and slid the door, along its rails, inside the wall of the Kart.

Once entering, Ruby sauntered farther in and sat down at one of the first cushioned seats that surrounded the inside walls of the Kart. Henry walked around the Portway door and entered the Kart. He crept further inside until he was face-to-face with the control panel built into the side wall of the Portway Kart.

Henry retrieved his Citizen Card from his back pocket and slid it halfway into a slot within the control panel. The backlit buttons began to emit light once the control panel was activated. Once operational, He withdrew his Citizen Card from the control panel and returned it to his back pocket.

Within the face of the control panel were a large lever switch, four buttons, and a speaker.

The two ends of the lever switch had different locations labeled. The top read "Central Hub" and the bottom read "Sanctuary."

Each of the four buttons was also labeled. The buttons read "Start, Stop, Open/Close Door, and Emergency" respectively. The word emergency was printed in a vibrant red, while the others were printed in deep black.

Henry reached up and pushed the "open/close door" button within the control panel.

Henry and Ruby both looked over as they could see the Portway door and the Portway Kart door now being closed by themselves. Once both doors had shut and become airtight within their frames, Henry then pushed the lever switch up toward the "Central Hub" label at the top.

Once the lever had been set to "Central Hub," the button labeled "Start" began to pulsate with light. Henry pressed the button in and felt the Kart begin to move.

Henry slowly walked through the Kart, trying to maintain balance as the movement along the tracks jostled him slightly. He staggered until he made it to a seat that sat across from Ruby.

"Hey, Henry? ..." Ruby asked.

"Yeah?" Henry asked in return.

"Since you and I are going to be stuck here for a while, why don't we make a pact?" Ruby suggested.

"A pact? What kind of pact?" Henry asked as he grew intrigued.

"We should look out for each other in case Charles gets, I don't know … too crazy or something. What do you say?" Ruby asked, half serious, half facetious.

Henry heard the question and felt a little anxious. He was now being asked to join a pact by the only girl he had ever liked for his whole life. The temptation was immense; It was near impossible for him to say no. Henry thought of how this would be a great start to his new working life.

"Sounds good to me," Henry agreed with a grin.

Ruby stuck out her hand, looking to complete a handshake. A huge smile was planted on her face.

Henry lifted his hand and grasped onto hers.

They shook in agreement. Henry and Ruby were now in a pact.

This was the start of their friendship.

Chapter 3

The Harbingers Of Fate

January 1st, 1994
9:32 PM
782 citizens exist

Henry sat against the base of a tree within the Sanctuary Dome. He puffed on his cigarette, feeling increasingly anxious about his impending first day of work.

As the cigarette had burned down to the filter he rubbed the lit ember against the bottom of his shoe until it extinguished. He stood up and flicked the filter out into the grass before stretching his back until it cracked. Henry then paused for a moment, taking in his scenery and pondering what his life was becoming.

As he thought to himself, Henry noticed in the shimmer of moonlight something was carved into the bark of a tree off in the distance.

Henry walked over and approached the tree. He saw the carving in the bark read "Life" with a hexagonal border surrounding the letters. He thought this was odd, but as he lifted his hand and felt the indentations in the wood, he took it as a possible good omen. Henry let the "Life" tree rest on the back burner of his mind, simmering. Finally concluding his thoughts, he decided to walk off toward Station 1.

9:58 PM

Henry had ventured amongst the trees until he was now at the face of the Station. As he stepped closer to the building, he saw Ruby and Charles sitting inside, awkwardly attempting conversation with one another. He walked over to the front door of Station 1 and pushed against the glass, letting himself inside. Once he had stepped through the doorway, Ruby and Charles both stopped talking and faced toward the door, staring at him.

"There he is! Come on in, my boy. Thought you might not show for a minute there; now we can get started!" Charles said emphatically.

Henry stepped farther into the room until he was at Charles' desk. He pulled on the back of the only empty chair and sat beside Ruby.

Charles stood up from his chair and disappeared into the back room of Station 1.

"Henry, let me grab your duffel bag, and I'll go over some more things before I send you two on your way," Charles stated from within the back room.

Henry glanced over and noticed a black duffel bag sitting on Ruby's lap.

Charles reentered the room, holding an identical duffel bag, and tossed it at Henry as he returned behind his desk.

Henry caught the bag in front of his face and sat it on his lap.

"Okay, only thing I really want to go over with you both face-to-face is how to use the radio," Charles said.

Charles reached over, unclipped the radio on his belt, and held it up so Henry and Ruby could see it.

"Go ahead and grab your radios inside your bags," Charles requested.

Henry and Ruby both unzipped their duffel bags and rummaged inside to retrieve their radios.

Henry pulled his radio out and rotated it around in his hand, studying the various dials and the button that controlled the small metal rectangle. He could see the radio had a speaker on the face, two small dials on top, a belt clip fastened to the back, and a red rectangular button on the right side.

"Ok, basically, this is the rundown. The dial with the yellow dot will select your channel. The channels you can choose from are A, B, and C. The dial with the white dot will choose your volume. Turn up the volume to listen to the channel. Turn down the volume all the way to shut off the radio. The red button on the side will allow you to speak to the channel. If you click it in and let go real fast, it will cause a chirp over the channel. Important reminder! You must say 'over' when you finish speaking. When the red button is pressed in, you will not be able to hear what is being said on the channel. Always stay on channel A, and never forget the importance of good radio etiquette. If you ever need new batteries, just let me know," Charles explained.

Charles stared at the pair for a moment.

"You got all that?" Charles asked.

Henry and Ruby both nodded their heads in agreement.

"Alright! That's what I like to see. Now for your first task, all I want you guys to do is to go find your Station and radio back to me once you get there. I'll explain more after that," Charles said.

Henry and Ruby both put their radios back into their duffel bags and zipped them shut. The pair stood up, each of them put the strap to the duffel bag onto their shoulders, and Ruby followed Henry as the pair made their way to the front door of Station 1. Henry grasped the metal handle of the door and stood behind it whilst he held it open to offer room for Ruby to walk through first. Once again, Ruby was flattered at the kind gesture and happily walked through. Henry was about to join her before being interrupted by Charles.

"Hey Henry, come here real quick!" Charles said.

Henry walked away from the door, leaving Ruby outside, and let it close behind him as he stepped back into the room.

"What is it?" Henry asked.

"It might make a better impression if you walk her to Station 3 first ... just a suggestion," Charles said with a wink.

"Noted," Henry said, feeling awkward about the unrequested advice.

Henry walked away from Charles and rejoined Ruby outside.

Henry and Ruby began to walk side by side amongst the trees as they traversed to their Stations. The pair walked for a couple of minutes until Ruby finally broke the silence.

"So, what did Mr. Ivory want?" Ruby asked.

"He said to try and be safe out here, watch out for the deer and stuff ..." Henry quickly lied.

"Well, that should be pretty easy, considering Charles is probably the most dangerous thing out here," Ruby said.

The pair began to laugh between themselves for a bit.

"Oh hey! I almost forgot!" Ruby said excitedly.

Henry watched as Ruby unzipped the top zipper to her duffel bag and began to rummage around inside. She pulled out a bright green glass bottle containing a scintillating emerald liquid and handed it to Henry.

"What's this?" Henry asked as he stared at the unfamiliar bottle Ruby placed in his hand.

"It's the soda I owe you from the jinx," Ruby said.

Henry rolled the bottle over in his palm so he could read the label.

"Green Genie Soda: a fortune under every cap!" was printed on the label in a vintage circus aesthetic surrounding the creepy smiling face of the genie mascot.

"Green Genie?" Henry questioned.

Ruby stuck her arm out and pressed her fingertips into the center of Henry's chest, effectively stopping his momentum. Both now stood alone out in the forest, surrounded by darkness and silence.

"Wait, you're not telling me you never had a *Green Genie* before, are you?" Ruby asked in shock.

"Can't say that I have," Henry said.

"I can't believe this. Someone in Cherry Blossom has never had a *Green Genie* before," Ruby said in disbelief.

"You make it seem like I never had soda before. I've had sodas, just not this one," Henry explained.

"Semantics, semantics, just open it. I want to know your fortune!" Ruby said with excitement.

"Alright," Henry agreed.

Henry twisted off the bottle cap and held it in his hand. He then lifted the bottle to his lips and took a big gulp of the soda. At first, Henry was drinking the *Green Genie* to prolong reading the fortune in order to slightly annoy Ruby, but as it turns out, when he tasted the beverage it was the best drink he had ever had in his life.

"Oh shit! That's really good," Henry said as he lowered the bottle before lifting it again to take another gulp.

"What's the fortune?! What's the fortune?!" Ruby asked, impatiently waiting.

Henry lowered the bottle from his mouth and consumed his gulp. He brushed the excess liquid from his lips and lifted the cap in his opposite hand. He then read it aloud.

"Do not feed into temptation ..." Henry said as he read what was printed.

"Ooh, sounds pretty ominous," Ruby said playfully.

"Welp, it's just some ink on a bottle cap," Henry said smugly.

"I don't know about that, Henry. These fortunes could very well predict your fate," Ruby further teased Henry.

"That's a bunch of malarkey," Henry said, impersonating Charles.

The pair began to laugh between themselves once again.

10:24 PM

Henry and Ruby continued to walk deeper into the forest until they arrived at Station 2.

"Alright, looks like this is your stop," Ruby said.

"Nah, I'll walk you to Station 3 first," Henry replied with confidence.

"Oh ... okay!" Ruby said with slight confusion that shifted to a happy acceptance.

Ruby felt butterflies begin to multiply rapidly in her stomach. For as much excitement as she felt inside, she kept an opposing calm demeanor on the surface.

10:46 PM

Henry and Ruby continued farther into the forest once again until they both arrived at Station 3.

"Guess this is your stop ..." Henry said jokingly, alluding to Ruby's earlier statement.

"Guess so ..." Ruby said, shying away from her emotions.

There was now an awkward silence filling the air between the pair. Both couldn't think of what to say. The romantic tension between them was axiomatic from afar. The tension soon dissipated once Henry spoke.

"Well ... uh, I guess I gotta head back to my Station ..." Henry said reluctantly.

"Yep ... " Ruby replied with the same tone of timorous affectation as Henry, further hiding deeper emotions under her exterior expression.

Henry turned away and slowly began to walk back toward Station 2.

Henry looked over his shoulder and back toward Ruby. He watched as she approached the front door of Station 3 and stepped inside the darkened building. When he knew she was inside safely, he directed his attention forward and continued his walk toward his Station.

"Ruby checking in. I'm at Station 3. Over," Ruby's muffled voice broadcasted out of the radio in Henry's duffel bag.

"Read you loud and clear. Over," Charles responded over the radio.

10:58 PM

Once Henry arrived at Station 2, he pushed on the glass of the front door and stepped inside the darkness. He removed the duffel bag from his shoulder and placed it on the floor of the Station. He bent down, unzipped the top zipper of the duffel bag, reached in, and retrieved the radio from inside. He held the radio in his hand, pressed the red button, and lifted the speaker to his mouth.

"Henry checking in. I made it to Station 2. Over," Henry said.

"Good to hear. Now, inside your duffel bags you'll both find the uniform along with various items for your belt. Go ahead, put everything on, and radio me back once you guys are done. Over," Charles said.

Henry looked around the darkened Station. On the far wall, he could see the faint silhouette of a light switch. Henry slid his radio into his unoccupied back pocket before he walked over to the switch and flicked it on. The lights overhead illuminated the Station, and he could now see everything in crisp detail. He noticed the desk inside Station 2 was out of place and pushed up against the back wall. Henry grabbed a leg of the desk and dragged it toward the center of the room. He then slid the desk so the right side was now touching the right wall.

Henry walked back and picked the duffel bag up off of the floor. He strolled over to the desk and placed the bag on top. Henry reached in and pulled out the uniform he felt inside. He lifted it up in front of himself and studied what he had to wear in the light.

The Sanctuary Park uniform was a dark olive green short-sleeved work shirt. On the right side of the shirt, Henry saw a tree logo with the name Sanctuary embroidered into the chest. Accompanying the shirt was a thick black long-sleeve, a thin utility belt, a flashlight, an emergency flare, and the park guide.

Henry thought about how it was strange that the uniform Charles wore differed from theirs. Charles' uniform was a dark olive green long-sleeve work shirt with a pocket stitched on the opposite side of his Sanctuary embroidery patch. He surmised that at some point, the Sanctuary uniforms had been updated in design and Charles' uniform had to be the old rendition of it.

Henry took off his jacket, letting it rest on the floor. He put on the black long-sleeve on top of the shirt he was currently wearing. He then put on the work shirt over the top of the black long-sleeve and buttoned it up. Henry removed his belt, placed it inside the duffel bag, and tucked all his shirts into his pants. He retrieved the thin utility belt from inside the bag, slid it into his belt loops, and strapped it around his waist. He began to sort the various items from his duffel bag into their respective places on his belt. He slid the flashlight into a metal ring that was fastened on the front right side of the belt. He then grabbed the emergency flare and began to inspect it. Henry read the finely printed instructions on the thin red tube and imagined how to ignite it as he read along, only having seen one used in instructional videos during Meltdown Preparation class. He felt around the belt until he found a snug leather pouch on the back right side. Henry slid the flare into the snug pouch and looked down at the belt, making sure everything was secure in its place. He then fully assessed what he was forced to wear for work. He adjusted and stretched the uniform around his torso until he felt everything fit correctly.

Henry lifted his radio out of his back pocket, held in the red button with his index finger, and spoke into the device.

"Got the uniform on. Over," Henry said.

The radio was silent for a minute.

"Got mine on. Over," Ruby said.

"Alright, now we're ready to start. The basic point of this job will be to prevent vandalism, dispose of trash, and do relative maintenance within the park. If you choose to walk around the park, do be mindful of the larger animals within; they are all herbivores, but they can still do a lot of harm if provoked. At the end of the summer we'll pull out the landscaping machinery behind Station 1 to do a clean sweep of all the overgrowth, then we'll ship those remains to the Farmlands. Tonight will be easy. All you gotta do is sit there and watch the park. Make sure there are no citizens in the Dome after hours. Follow the rules laid out in the guides I gave you, and have a safe night. Over," Charles said.

Henry clipped the radio to his belt and tried to find a chair to sit in. He searched around the room for a quick second but couldn't find anything. He noticed that the only place he hadn't searched yet was the back room of the Station.

Henry walked over, twisted the handle, and opened the door to the back room. Once the door had revealed the room beyond, all he could see inside was a dimly lit void. Henry slowly peered his head into the back room and saw the room was barren beside the door to the bathroom being on the left wall. All other walls were blank and empty.

Set in the right corner of the room were six spare ARS filters stacked next to a lonely roller chair that was tipped over on its side.

Henry stepped inside the room and picked the chair up off the ground. He walked out into the main room of the Station and set the chair behind the desk. He sat down and kicked up his feet, resting them atop the desk. He stared out the front window paneling of the Station and deep into the forest.

Henry was now stuck at work with nothing to do for nine hours.

He spent the first two hours thinking about his life and periodically smoking cigarettes. Henry would eventually rest his head, within his folded arms, over the desk and drift off to sleep for the remainder of his shift.

7:00 AM

"Alright! You kids have completed your first day of work! Go home, get some rest, and I'll see you guys tonight. Over," Charles announced over the radio.

Henry was startled awake by Charles' uproar. He slowly sat up from the desk and wiped the drool from his face. He struggled to rise to his feet, grabbing hold of his duffel bag and jacket with the little strength he had. With his belongings in hand, he then sauntered over to the back of the Station to turn off the overhead lights.

Henry exited Station 2, leaving it dark and grim. He slowly proceeded to walk through the forest back to the Portway door.

7:24 AM

Henry walked along the grass as he fed his addiction and puffed away on a cigarette. Once he had sight of the Portway door he could see Ruby standing alone next to the Portway call button, almost as if she was waiting for him.

Henry walked toward Ruby, and once he was within hearing distance, she called out to him.

"Hey! How was the night for you?" Ruby asked.

"Eh, it was alright. Whole lot of nothing … How about you?" Henry responded.

"Yeah, it was fine, nothing either. Saw a deer a couple times, so that was pretty cool," Ruby playfully answered.

"You sure it wasn't a citizen? Hate to see you slacking on the job already," Henry said with heavy sarcasm as he met and stood next to Ruby.

Ruby saw the cigarette in Henry's mouth and decided she was going to be coy. She reached over and gently removed the cigarette from his lips and placed it into hers. She began to puff on Henry's cigarette as she continued the conversation with a smugness as if she was the rightful owner of the cancer stick.

"You never know; with all the ugly people like you living in Blossom, it very well could have been," Ruby said with heavier sarcasm.

"Fuck off! I'm gorgeous," Henry said in fake arrogance as he chuckled.

The pair laughed together and enjoyed each other's presence.

Ruby smacked the Portway call button with the bottom of her fist and activated it. The sound of a bell rang out from the speaker within the Portway door's frame.

Henry watched as Ruby did this and slowly came to the realization that she actually was waiting for him. He felt happily surprised by Ruby's actions but decided to just keep his thoughts to himself. He didn't want to put so much emphasis on such a small action.

Soon, the Portway Kart arrived and made itself flush with the Portway door. Once an airtight seal was established, the speaker within the Portway door's frame broadcasted a loud buzzer.

Ruby smoked the cigarette down to the filter and rubbed the remainder against the bottom of her shoe to extinguish it. She slid the filter into her pocket and grasped her hands over one another behind her back before rocking slightly in place as she waited.

Henry stepped over toward the hatch wheel in the center of the Portway door and spun it until the door unlocked. He gripped the hatch wheel and pulled on it until the Portway door opened to its fullest extent. Henry walked around the Portway door and stepped inside to unlock the Portway Kart door. Once he unlocked the Kart door, he slid it along its rails out of the way.

Henry stepped in and from inside the doorway of the Kart, he stuck his head out parallel to the floor, hiding his lower half, and looked back at Ruby.

"Our chariot awaits!" Henry said in a hyperbolic fancy accent.

Ruby giggled, lightly pushing Henry's head back and out of the way as she stepped inside the Portway Kart.

The pair traversed back to the Homelands Dome; each said goodbye to one another and went their separate ways home, soon to return that same night.

Chapter 4

The Vanishing

January 3rd, 1994
9:55 PM
781 citizens remain

A somber eeriness fell over the town of Cherry Blossom. A thick blanket of sadness coated existence, palpable to the senses.

Henry stood alone in the Portway Kart, waiting for the Kart to become flush with the Portway door to Sanctuary. As he stared out both windows of the Portway Kart and the Portway door, he could see blurred movement on the other side. Once the Kart created an airtight seal with the Dome door, Henry submerged his finger into the "open/close door" button and was greeted with familiar metallic booms. The Portway door finally unlocked itself and slowly swung open.

Standing on the opposite side of the Kart door was Ruby. She locked eyes with Henry as he unlocked the Kart door, slid it open into the Kart wall, and stepped out into Sanctuary. She took off the headphones on her head and paused the cassette player clipped on her belt.

"Hey. What are you doing here? Shouldn't you be at the Station?" Henry asked.

"Well, I can either do nothing over there or do nothing over here. Plus, I figured that we could walk together," Ruby said.

"Oh, okay!" Henry said, delighted.

Ruby retrieved her radio from her belt. She lifted the device up to her mouth as she held in the red button to speak.

"Henry and I are in the Dome, heading to our Stations now. Over," Ruby stated into the radio toward Charles.

"Good to hear. Keep safe and be on the lookout tonight. … I'm sure by now you guys know why. Over," Charles stated.

The pair began to walk along the dirt trail toward their Stations as they further conversed.

"What was Charles talking about?" Henry asked Ruby.

"You didn't hear?" Ruby asked.

"Hear what?" Henry asked in return.

"Janine Crane has gone missing. Nobody has seen her," Ruby said.

"Oh no. That's awful," Henry said, surprised and distraught.

"Yeah, they said she just vanished," Ruby explained.

"Well, that explains the EGC (Emergency Gas Control) all over the Central Hub just now. Seems like the secret tunnels have been discovered. I guess The Tunnel Society finally made it out," Henry said.

"It's just so weird; why would anyone want to escape? You think there could be something out there for them? Another safe haven we don't know about?" Ruby pondered to Henry.

"I don't know. Maybe there is. Maybe once she got out, she couldn't find her way back. Personally, I can't understand why anyone would join the society in the first place. Seems like a lost cause," Henry said

"What? You scared of huffin' a lil' bit of Ultra-18? Nah, I see what you mean, though. All I know is that ever since the new year started, life in Cherry Blossom has gotten pretty strange and it's only been three days. What if the rumors are true? What if there really is a 'double decade curse?' What if, for the first time ever, we have a real-life murder mystery on our hands? Just like the movies! Anyone could be a suspect. What if it's Charles? What if it's Ted Williams? It could even be you, Henry. Don't think that bland exterior of yours is hiding anything," Ruby playfully pondered, teasing Henry as she tried to make light of the ordeal.

"The only thing I'm scared of is that you've already huffed too much. Eh, I don't know though. Charles *is* crazy, but murder? He's just a weird drunk geezer. Doesn't seem like he'd ever be sober enough to do it. Ted is more of a graffiti and arson kind of guy, not murder. ... and me? Well, you better watch yourself, Jenkins. I know I made a pact with you, but what will I do when it's just us two left? In all seriousness, when I woke up today, something just felt so ... strange, ya know? I'm not superstitious or anything, but only a couple days into the new year and someone has vanished for the first time? Sounds like a curse to me. I'm probably going to be seeing some weird shit in my dreams tonight," Henry said, entertaining Ruby's theory while sarcastically taunting her.

"Wait, You've been sleeping at work?" Ruby asked.

"Yep, getting credits to snooze on the job. Easy earnings! Although, my back has been killing me lately. You're telling me you don't get bored sitting out here all night?" Henry asked.

"I usually just listen to my music and think ... but if you're so bored ... why not just radio me?" Ruby nervously suggested.

"You really would wanna talk on the radio all night?" Henry asked, surprised.

"Yeah, why not?" Ruby asked, playfully optimistic.

"Won't Charles hear us?" Henry questioned.

"We can talk on channel C!" Ruby said with a smile.

10:27 PM

Henry and Ruby continued to converse as they walked through the forest until they arrived at Station 3.

"Well, we're here!" Henry said.

"Indeed we are," Ruby agreed.

Ruby walked away from Henry and pushed open the front door to the Station. She stood in the doorway as she looked back out toward him.

"Well, I guess I will see you in the morning," Henry said, slightly reluctant.

"I guess you will ... I'll be on channel C," Ruby said with a seductive gaze before stepping inside Station 3 and shutting the door behind herself.

Ruby quickly stepped away from view in the glass panels and disappeared into the back room of Station 3, hiding her excitement and blushing face.

Henry watched as she did this and thought it was odd, but he was too focused on the way she said, "I'll be on channel C," He replayed the memory in his head over and over again, his whole journey back to Station 2.

10:41 PM

Once Henry stepped inside Station 2, he unclipped the radio from his belt, walked over, and placed it on the desk. He paced around the center of the room for a moment while his mind ran rampant with hypothetical scenarios of how talking to Ruby on the radio might go. Soon, Henry became overwhelmed with all the possibilities in his mind and he ceased his pacing. He closed his eyes and took in a long and powerful inhale. He held his breath until he could feel the stress wilting away from his body. Henry exhaled and collected himself. He felt as prepared as he could at this moment.

Henry turned and looked over at the radio placed on the desk. He slowly stepped toward it and nervously grasped the device in his hand. He began to sweat slightly as he twisted the channel dial over to "C." Henry took another deep breath before finally clicking in the red button and lifting the speaker to his mouth.

"Hello?" Henry asked with curiosity.

"Hey! Was thinking you fell asleep on me already," Ruby said.

"How could I fall asleep on the first night I had something to look forward to?" Henry responded.

1:48 AM

As the pair talked over the radio, Henry started to crave a cigarette. He retrieved a fresh cigarette and a lighter from his jacket pocket, stepped outside Station 2, and sparked the stress relief.

Henry walked away from Station 2, smoking and talking to Ruby over the radio, meandering around the forest. He eventually wandered deeper into Sanctuary toward the back of the Dome.

2:13 AM

"So, What are you going to do with your credits first?" Ruby asked.

"I don't know, I'm thinking I might save up for a TV in my room. Something cool like that. What about you?" Henry asked.

"I'm definitely buying more cassettes, need more music in my life," Ruby answered.

"Oh cool, like what?" Henry asked, intrigued.

"There's this band called *StarChild*; they used to make like hardcore rock and stuff. There's a couple of their albums I haven't heard yet. Can't wait till I can," Ruby said.

"You'll have to show me their stuff sometime," Henry added.

"Will do. More people need to appreciate *StarChild*. They always have a song for every occasion," Ruby stated.

"Is that your favorite band?" Henry inquired further.

"Hmm nah. I think *Soul Stone* might be my favorite, but the more I listen to *StarChild*, the more I like them, so maybe one day, we'll have to wait and see. How about you? What music do you like?" Ruby asked in return.

"I'm weird when it comes to music; I like songs that make me feel sorta ... despondent. *Undead Skeletons* is a really good band for that. If I'm in the mood, I'll listen to a song and repeatedly play it for hours on end. Squeezing every ounce of feeling I can out of it," Henry answered.

"Oh wow, I didn't know you knew *Undead Skeletons*. They're in my top 5 for sure," Ruby said, pleasantly surprised.

"Oh yeah, I've been listening to them since ... I ... was ... 7. Uh, Ruby? I'm going to have to radio you back," Henry said as his tone changed from happy to uneased.

"What's the matter?" Ruby asked, slightly concerned.

"I see someone in the Dome. I gotta go yell at 'em," Henry said unenthusiastically.

"Oh, ok. Well, stay safe out there," Ruby said.

At this moment, Henry stood 80 meters away from the mausoleum as he saw a citizen knelt down in the grass, hunched over, 10 meters from the structure. He returned his radio to his belt as he stepped closer to the stranger.

The figure was obscured by the shadows cast from the trees in the moonlight, keeping their identity hidden. Henry crept closer within earshot before he made his presence known.

"Hey! You can't be in this Dome after hours!" Henry shouted as he cupped his hands by his mouth.

The unknown person turned their head to look back toward Henry. Within the darkened silhouette of the figure, He could only see their pupils reflecting glimmered beams of cerulean moonlight at him before quickly turning away once they caught sight of him.

The stranger broke off into a full sprint, running away from Henry and toward the mausoleum door.

"Hey! Stop! Get back to the Portway!" Henry shouted further.

The mysterious individual reached the mausoleum door, opened it, and slammed it behind themselves as they entered.

Henry gave chase until he was at the door to the Crypt. He gripped the latch, ratcheted it unlocked, and swung the door open with intense force. He stepped inside the Crypt and to the edge of the metal railing located at the top landing of the stone spiral staircase. He peered over the railing and stared down into a black void.

Henry retrieved his flashlight from his belt, clicked it on, and shined it down into the depths below. As the light illuminated the bottom of the Crypt, Henry caught a glimpse of a feminine arm slithering and slipping under the sewer grate in the center of the floor, accompanied by a loud metal thud as the grate fell back into its socket.

"Fuckin' dumbass Tunnel Society," Henry said under his breath in distaste.

Henry walked away from the encounter and stepped out of the mausoleum. He shut the door behind himself as he left the Crypt and walked back the way he came. He cast the light outward down upon his path and took a couple of steps forward before he saw something out on the ground ahead. Henry stepped closer until he was looking down, glaring over what was lying in the grass.

Henry now stood before the top half of a rabbit's carcass, completely severed from its missing lower half, oozing guts and blood out of its open stomach encapsulated by the light.

"What a sick asshole," Henry said in appalled disgust.

Henry retrieved the radio from his belt. He lifted the speaker to his mouth and held down the red button.

"Ruby, you there?" Henry asked.

"Hey, what's up?" Ruby asked.

"It was just one of the Tunnelers being a disgusting fuck," Henry explained.

"What makes you say that?" Ruby asked curiously.

Henry continued to stare at the slain rabbit before him. He struggled to find the words to inform Ruby of what currently plagued his vision.

"Apparently, Charles isn't the only one eating the rodents in Sanctuary ..." Henry stated.

Henry and Ruby would converse over the radio for the remaining hours of their shift.

At 7:00 AM, Henry would walk Ruby from Station 3, out of the Sanctuary Dome, back inside the Homelands Dome, and finally back to her house.

Henry felt as if his friendship with Ruby was growing into something more, but he couldn't really tell if it was real or if his twisted delusions and lust for love were convincing him his hyperbolic fantasies were coming true. Only time could tell.

Chapter 5

The Hunt

January 17th, 1994
12:45 PM
775 citizens remain

The color of the sky was a dreary gray. Rain fell against the Sanctuary Dome with an audible trickle unheard by those inside.

A gunshot echoed throughout the trees.

A girl ran through the forest in a frightened haste, a single streak of blood dripping from the side of her mouth.

This was Amy McCardinal. She was 20 years old, had long, straight black hair with short, boxed bangs, was a member of The Tunnel Society, and loved photography; always seen taking pictures all over Cherry Blossom for her personal collection and enjoyment. She currently wore her power plant coverall uniform and was disheveled all over.

Amy ran through Sanctuary, frantically looking over her back, trying to catch sight of the man chasing her. She panicked within herself as she was being hunted.

She ran until she chose a tree to hide behind and rested her back against the bark, out of sight of her pursuer. She waited against the trunk, trying to catch her breath before he called out to her.

"You can't fool me!!! …" Charles screamed gutturally out into the forest.

When she heard him antagonize her, Amy froze in fear. She turned over and slowly stuck her head out from behind the tree, peering around the bark. When she stared back into the forest, she could see Charles, wearing an EGO gas mask and bright yellow arm-length rubber gloves, persistently checking behind trees and waving around a *Serpent Slayer .35* revolver he held in his hand.

Amy stared at Charles as he inspected the immediate area around him before he glanced over, froze within his movement, and saw her face fearfully watching him from behind the tree. Charles swiftly pointed his revolver toward her and fired. His quick movement of the gun caused his aim to be off and he struck the center of the tree.

Once the bullet collided with the bark, a small crevice was created in the trunk. Amy submerged deeper in her fear by the bullet being fired in her direction and chose to flee.

Amy sprinted away from the tree and darted behind another.

"… There's no hiding now! I saw your eyes! … I know it's you!!!" Charles shouted at Amy, taunting her as she ran away.

Charles ran after her and around the tree she had disappeared behind. Stepping out from behind the tree Charles saw Amy running away down a narrow path of the forest.

Charles raised his revolver and had a clear shot.

He pulled the trigger and the gun fired.

"Aaaaaaaahhhhhh!!!" Amy screamed out as she was struck.

The bullet entered Amy's torso and lodged in her body. She fell to the grass and dirt below. She began to bleed heavily, staining her uniform as she was pulling herself forward, crawling along the grass toward the base of a tree in front of her.

Amy pulled herself forward a final time before she turned over on her back, laid partially against the roots of the tree, and watched as Charles slowly sauntered toward her, loading more bullets into his revolver until the cylinder was full.

Charles took a final step forward and stood in front of Amy, three meters away from her. He flicked the cylinder back into the revolver, gave it a powerful spin, and waited until it had stopped with a bullet lined up with the hammer. He lifted the gun and aimed the barrel at Amy's heart.

"No more …" Charles said with soft, vile hatred.

Amy gave Charles a final look of hopeless defeat.

Charles pulled the trigger again.

A gunshot rang out into the Sanctuary Dome.

Blood splattered against the tree.

Amy's arms fell limp by her sides.

Her body began to leak profusely, staining the grass and soil beneath her in a small puddle.

Charles waited for a moment. He stared at Amy's body, watching for any movement, sorrowfully basking in the sight of the deceased woman lying before himself.

Charles finally decided to slide the revolver between his waistband and lower back. He took slow steps in the grass as he made his way toward Amy's corpse, removing a folded plastic tarp from his back pocket as he got closer to her.

Once at her body, he carefully undid and laid the tarp parallel along Amy. Charles positioned himself at her side, knelt down, and carefully pushed Amy, rolling her over onto the tarp. Once she was placed, lying motionless, atop the plastic sheeting, Charles began wrapping her up until she was fully enclosed and preserved. Charles then carefully slid his glove-adorned hands underneath Amy's swathing, lifting her from the ground beneath.

Charles walked off, holding Amy in his arms, toward the Crypt.

1:53 PM

Charles opened the Crypt door and stared into the darkness inside.

He clicked on the light embedded within his EGO gas mask and cast an orange-tinged clarity that cut through the darkness.

Charles returned to Amy's body on the ground next to him. He lifted her again, stepped inside the Crypt, and slowly lowered himself down the stone spiral staircase.

Once at the bottom, he walked over toward an open slot meant for a casket within the cobblestone walls and knelt down in front of it. He slid Amy's body inside the cutout and pushed her as far as he could into the opening. Once he had placed her body into position, Charles turned around, stepped over toward the last step at the bottom of the staircase, and began removing the stones that created it. He placed the large stones over the opening, holding Amy until it was fully covered.

Once he finished his construction, Charles rested against the wall, panting from his efforts.

"Don't worry … I've got plans for you …" Charles said as he patted the wall of stones he created.

He left the Crypt, proud of what he had done and was planning to do, nonchalantly walking back to Station 1.

2:46 PM

Charles stepped inside Station 1. He removed his EGO gas mask and gloves, setting them on his desk as he crept farther into the room.

Charles turned and walked over to the rotary phone attached in the center of the farthest wall.

Charles picked up the handset and put the receiver to his ear. He rotated the dial and entered 000. The line rang a few times before someone answered.

"Peace Officers. Where is your Emergency?" the operator asked.

"Sanctuary Dome. We have a puddle of blood out here. Just like the others," Charles answered.

"Damn ... that makes four Domes affected now ... Okay, an officer is on the way! Be ready to hand over your Citizen Card for Portway record inquiries," the operator informed Charles.

"Will do," Charles stated.

Charles slowly hung up the phone and glanced over at a section of floorboards in the corner of Station 1. He turned and stepped over toward the spot he was fixated on. He crouched down and began removing the unsecured floorboards that covered a hidden compartment underneath the wood.

Charles stood up from the ground and sauntered over to the desk. He gathered his gloves and EGO gas mask, brought them over, and stored them in the darkness underneath the floorboards. Charles then retrieved his gun from his waistband and studied it for a moment. He glanced down into the darkened corridor at a duffel bag lying at the bottom, contemplating his plans for what rested inside.

Charles reached in and laid his revolver down on top of the duffel bag. He returned the floorboards to their original housing before he stood and began mentally preparing himself to be investigated.

3:54 PM

Peace Officer Ernest Rodney was 45 years old, tall, lanky and had a well-trimmed dark walnut mustache. He was currently wearing his Peace Officer uniform, utility belt with a Peace Officer pistol holstered within it, silver framed aviator glasses, and had a DRD (Data Retrieval Device) strapped over his shoulder resting at his side.

He was crouched down in the grass, staring at the blood stain that lay in between the cones and tape he just placed around the tree. He smoked his cigarette in a curious ponder.

Officer Rodney stood up, slid the roll of crime tape into his jacket pocket, and put his finger to his chin.

"Hmmm. That's odd …" Officer Rodney stated as he removed the cigarette from his mouth.

"What is?" Charles asked.

"Well, all the other disappearance stains were big blood puddles with little splashes here and there, but this? This is more concentrated … smaller puddle and a larger splatter instead. It's just odd. I think the killer might be changing their method of attack," Officer Rodney explained to Charles.

There was a moment of silence between the two.

Officer Rodney put his hands behind his back and turned to Charles, who stood next to him.

"Hey, Mr. Ivory? I'd hate to ask, but I just gotta cover all my bases … can I see your Citizen Card?" Officer Rodney requested with fake awkwardness.

"I understand … here ya go," Charles said as he retrieved his Citizen Card from his person and held it out to him.

Officer Rodney gripped the DRD in its leather carrying case and rotated it around his waist until it hung down in front of him. He returned the cigarette to his mouth, took Charles' Citizen Card from him and slid it halfway into the thin slot on the face of the dense rectangular device built below its screen. The small green and black monochrome monitor on the face of the device activated, displaying Charles' Portway logs, his Credits balance, his occupation, his address, and his age. Officer Rodney used the small toggle stick and two tactile buttons built below the monitor to maneuver through Charles' personal data, looking for any inconsistencies in his alibi.

After a vigorous scan of Charles' Portway logs, Officer Rodney turned to him with a confused look on his face.

"You haven't been out of the Sanctuary Dome in almost a month?" Officer Rodney asked.

"Yep. Only leave to get stocked up on booze every so often. Gotta tell ya, It's a bitch gettin' it all here in one trip ... but I manage," Charles stated.

"What do you do for food?" Officer Rodney asked as he removed his cigarette.

"Well ... uh, I stock up on storable foods on my liquor runs. I've actually grown to like the *EZ-Cook Noodles* a lot now," Charles explained.

"Hmm ... ok, well, why do you stay here?" Officer Rodney asked whilst waving the lit cigarette in his fingers.

"If I told you, you wouldn't believe me," Charles stated in a defeated tone.

"Oh, don't tell me it's that stupid monster story again, Charles; you already wasted my time with that shit a month ago," Officer Rodney said in angry annoyance.

"I knew you wouldn't believe me," Charles plainly stated.

Officer Rodney withdrew Charles' Citizen Card from the DRD and handed it back to him, giving him a disapproving look. Charles took his Citizen Card back and returned it to his pocket in a spiteful manner.

"Ok. Charles, you're clear. If you hear or see anything out here again, you know how to reach me. Ease up on the boozin' and have a safe night ..." Officer Rodney said as he turned to his side and began to walk off toward the Portway door.

Officer Rodney took a few steps forward and then stopped within his momentum. He spun around in place and faced Charles again.

"Oh! And Charles, whatever you do, don't go telling Henry and Ruby that monster story. Ok?" Officer Rodney requested.

Charles gave Officer Rodney a disgruntled stare.

"Yeah, yeah!" Charles said, pissed off, as he waved his hand, shooing him away.

Officer Rodney spun back around, returned the cigarette to his mouth and continued toward the Portway door.

8:30 PM

Charles walked toward the Mausoleum, finally gaining the courage to enact his plan after ingesting copious amounts of alcohol. He stumbled forward in a drunken stupor, looking down at the syringe and bottle of *Magma Mouth Spiced Whiskey* he held in his hands, anxiously wanting to take a sample of Amy's blood.

Charles looked up from the noxious objects in his hands and caught sight of the Crypt out ahead of him, almost 50 meters away. He stood in worried shock as he gazed upon the mausoleum door and saw small amounts of Ultra-18 seeping out from it. Charles dropped the syringe and bottle, letting them shatter in the grass beneath him, out of fear.

Chapter 6

The Side Effects Of War

January 17th, 1994
9:48 PM
775 Citizens remain

Henry and Ruby stood side by side in the Sanctuary Dome as they both gazed upon the grass and dirt that sat before them in the clarity of Henry's flashlight.

The pair stared fearfully at the bloodstain Charles had created, not knowing he was the cause. The sight of someone's viscus remnants splattered upon the bark stained their eyes and soldered to their memory.

Henry and Ruby were fixated on what they saw showcased out in front of them. They felt appalled and nervous by this display of horror.

Henry noticed something in the apex of his vision that caught his attention.

Once he glanced up and understood what he was staring at, Henry became disturbed and lifted the light to shine it upon the tree. As the flashlight illuminated the bark he could see it even clearer. This was the "Life" tree.

Shortly below the "Life" etching was a missing poster for Robert Schafer that Charles had stapled to the tree just a few days prior.

Blood had been painted up the bark, partially covering both the poster and the etching. Henry's possible good omen had been disfigured into something he now saw as morbid and cruel of existence itself.

Robert's sinister smile and innocent eyes in the photo, covered in blood, stared back at Henry, plaguing him in morose turmoil. This sight hindered Henry's hope for humanity.

As the pair watched over the scene their attention was taken by Charles' voice coming out of the radio.

"Henry and Ruby? Come in. Over," Charles announced over the radio.

Henry reached over and unclipped the radio from his belt. He lifted the speaker to his mouth and held down the red button.

"Ruby and I are inside Sanctuary, just came across the cones. Over," Henry said in a saddened tone.

"Yeah … unfortunately, times are gettin' worse around here. Both you and Ruby report to Station 1. We need to discuss some things. Over," Charles requested.

Once they heard Charles' request Henry and Ruby both looked away from the scene and made eye contact. A deep, unwavering sense of dread began to intensify between them.

10:01 PM

The pair walked mournfully through the forest toward Station 1.

Every tree that surrounded Henry and Ruby on their journey was adorned with a missing poster containing the smiling face of someone they had once known.

The pair averted their eyes from the sea of posters belonging to the presumed deceased. The vanished stared back menacingly at them. They continued as such through Sanctuary until they arrived at Station 1.

10:17 PM

Henry and Ruby sat in silence as Charles stared at the pair with a look of concern from beyond his desk. The silence permeated and coated the inner walls of Station 1 until it was finally broken when Charles cleared his throat and spoke softly.

"I know things are looking bad ... these days are the worst they've been yet in this town ... now with more and more people getting eaten, and this encounter in Sanctuary no less, things are gettin' too close for comfort," Charles stated.

"Wait, getting eaten? What are you talking about?" Ruby questioned Charles.

"Oh, now don't fool yourself. Don't get me wrong, I believed it was some crazed citizen killing people at first as well, but this is much worse than that," Charles explained

Henry and Ruby both slowly turned their heads toward one another and gave each other a look of worry.

The pair turned back and Henry stared into Charles' eyes. He gazed deep into the black void and knew what looked back were the eyes of a deranged man.

"Charles, explain what you mean," Henry requested.

"I need to tell you kids a story …" Charles began to explain.

Henry and Ruby stared at Charles with anticipation, waiting to hear what he would conjure up in his twisted delusions.

"There's an Epigone out there …" Charles further explained.

"A what?" Ruby asked.

"It's an Epigone … a horrific shapeshifting creature created from a byproduct of humanity's lust for destruction …" Charles alluded.

Henry and Ruby both sat back, stunned; permanent looks of confusion plagued their faces.

"What? …" Henry struggled to ask.

"During my stay in the army, there was a year when the gas bombings were constant …" Charles said.

"Oh! The gas attacks of '71?" Ruby abruptly asked.

"Exactly. During this time, a lot of our men came back over exposed and I was assigned to assist in the medical tents where I was stationed. While assisting there, I witnessed almost every stage of gas poisoning there is. The worst I had ever seen was one man who was … macabre. Possibly the single worst thing I would ever witness during my time. He was lost in the gas for years before someone finally found him. Somehow, he was still alive. I have seen horrific things and he was the definition of horrifying. We had to keep him away from the other patients. His skin was … so … amorphous. It wasn't even a week before one of the nurses was attacked. ... She was partially being eaten alive before we could finally stop him. We couldn't save her in time. ... We had to end both of their suffering. After that, someone in the platoon gave him the moniker and it stuck. The worst exposure side effect there is ... becoming an Epigone," Charles told.

"Okay, so ... you think someone huffed some '18' and started killing and eating people?" Ruby questioned.

"No, no, no, this is different. This thing ain't human anymore ... Think about the evidence left behind, the pools of blood, the tunnels in the sewers, no bodies ever recovered; there's no way anyone could kill so many people under these Dome walls and not get caught by now. It's feeding on the citizens. Eating them whole. Someone or something outside the Domes must have turned and dug its way in," Charles explained.

"So ... instead of a person, you think it's a ... shapeshifting creature? ... What makes you say that?" Henry asked.

"It's a doppelgänger ... has a horrifying defense mechanism. It's always hiding in plain sight ... When we went to stop the nurse from being attacked, the soldier eating her somehow mutated his skin to look identical to her, clothes and all. Although it had slight ... defects. I've never seen anything like it ... that's why no one has been caught yet. It could look like anyone. If it tastes your blood, it could even look just like you ..." Charles answered.

When Charles explained this to Henry and Ruby, they couldn't take him seriously. Charles' story broke the bounds of what was possible by reality and was too impractical to be even considered real for a second.

"Charles, why are you telling us this?" Henry questioned pragmatically.

"With this most recent disappearance happening inside Sanctuary, I've decided to take precautions to help keep us all safe and secure," Charles said.

Charles slid his chair away from his desk.

Resting on the ground next to Charles' foot was a duffel bag. Charles bent down and unzipped the top zipper of the bag. He reached inside and slowly pulled out a *Westmoreland Crater-MakerVII* shotgun. He held it up in both hands so the pair could clearly see the weapon, pointing the barrel in a safe direction.

Henry and Ruby, never having been this close in the presence of a gun before, both equally became incredibly nervous and intensely intrigued at the first sight of a shotgun in real life.

"Is that a gun? No fucking way! Where'd you get it?" Henry asked in excited disbelief.

"This beauty right here is one of a couple of little souvenirs I kept from the outside world before moving into Cherry Blossom. Wasn't going to let some 'no citizen gun policy' stop me. This was my most cherished secret; now I'm trusting both of you to take care of it and use it responsibly," Charles said.

"Yes, sir," Henry said.

"Will do!" Ruby said.

"Now let me show you guys how to properly operate this thing. First, you need a shell …" Charles started to explain.

Charles slid his fingers into his shirt pocket and pulled out a single red shotgun shell. Charles then took the gun and angled it so Henry and Ruby could see the loading gate on the bottom of the frame.

"You take your ammo, like so, and you load it into the loading gate down here. Put your thumb on the gold bit of the shell and just slide it along this metal bit till it's inside this tube, as such. You can fit about five shells total in here. You take the forestock up here, slide it back, then forward again to load the shell into the chamber. … Just like that. Keep the chamber clear and the barrel pointed in a safe direction at all times unless you intend to kill something," Charles demonstrated as he spoke.

Charles gripped the shotgun in both hands. He tilted the gun to the side so the ejection port was facing toward the ceiling. Charles racked the forestock and sent the shell in the chamber, out of the ejection port, into the air. The shell twirled with momentum before Charles reached out and caught it in front of himself. Charles then paused for a moment before he glanced over and tossed the shell at Henry.

Henry lifted his hand and caught the shell.

"Give it a go, Henry …" Charles said.

Charles slowly rested the shotgun on the desk. He sat back and waited for Henry to pick it up.

Henry slowly stood up from his chair. He lurked over the desk, observing the weapon that lay before him. He hesitantly lifted his hand and grasped onto the gun.

Clenching onto the center of the weapon, Henry lifted it and turned it upside down. Henry took the shell in his hand and repeated Charles' actions to reload the gun. Henry pressed his thumb against the back of the shell, sliding it along the loading gate and into the feeding tube. He flipped the gun right side up and held it by both grips. Henry racked the forestock of the shotgun and successfully loaded a shell into the chamber.

Henry inspected the gun as he became more intrigued by it.

"Now, let's do some target practice," Charles said.

"Really?" Henry asked, staring at Charles in further excited disbelief.

"Yep, go outside and pick a tree," Charles said.

Henry looked away from Charles and out the Station windows, casting his vision onto the dense forest, until he chose the closest tree he could see rooted in front of Station 1.

Henry gave Ruby a quick glance of excitement before stepping away from the desk and out the front door of the Station.

Henry slowly approached the tree he selected and left distance between him and the trunk. He lifted the stock of the gun and planted it firmly into his shoulder. He tried to replicate how he had seen a shotgun operated in movies. Henry lifted the barrel up and pointed it at the tree. He slid his finger over the trigger and pulled against it.

Inside the gun, the firing pin swung forward, struck the shell, and ignited an explosion inside the barrel. The shotgun spewed a bright array of sparks and fire as the projectile contained in the shell erupted from inside and collided into the tree with tremendous exertion.

Henry felt the recoil of the gun push the backstock against his shoulder and stumbled backward as he tried to maintain control over the weapon. The projectile struck the tree and ripped the bark from its exterior, leaving a hand-sized crater in its place. The immediate air surrounding the trunk was flooded with sawdust and wood fibers.

The sound of the shotgun firing ricocheted off of Sanctuary's Dome walls and reverberated back into Henry's ears over five times before the noise deafened back to silence.

Henry turned away from the tree and began to walk back to Station 1. As Henry stepped inside the Station, he caught a glimpse of Ruby's eyes staring at him with a lustful gaze before she quickly put on a new face. Henry slid the strap connected to the shotgun over his head and let the gun rest across his back as he stepped farther into the Station.

"Great work, my boy! Glad to see you get the hang of it so fast. Now listen, this weapon stays in this Dome at all times. When you're done using it, store it in your Station's back room, out of plain sight. … Now, since you know how to use it, I need your help," Charles said.

"What do you need me to do?" Henry asked.

"Out at the Crypt, there's a gas leak seeping through; can't let that creature have an open door inside the Dome. Need your help to patch it up; I want you to cover my back so I ain't eaten next," Charles explained.

"Ok, sounds simple enough," Henry agreed.

"Ruby, I need you to wait outside the Crypt and make sure nothing comes in after us," Charles continued to explain.

"Ok, not a problem," Ruby agreed.

"Good ..." Charles said.

Charles stood up from his chair. He reached around to his backside and gripped the *Serpent Slayer .35* revolver secured between his shirt and waistband. Charles pulled his hand out from behind his back and revealed the revolver to Henry and Ruby. Charles lifted his thumb and fully cocked back the gun's hammer while the barrel was pointed at the ceiling. He stared at Henry and Ruby with an intense look of determination.

"... Let's ride!" Charles said.

Chapter 7

The Execution Hour

January 18th, 1994
10:37 PM
775 citizens remain

Henry and Charles stood side by side in Sanctuary Park, staring at the mausoleum 40 meters in front of them; both were equipped wearing Sanctuary's EGO gas masks. Henry gripped tight onto the shotgun as he gazed upon the small building. Charles firmly held his revolver in one hand and had an LCD strapped to his back.

The concrete structure gave Henry an uneasy feeling by sight alone. Henry could see green vapors of Ultra-18 seeping out of the cracks of the mausoleum door, giving it an ominous allure.

"You ready, Henry?" Charles asked.

"Ready as I'll ever be," Henry sarcastically answered.

"Alright then, lights on," Charles instructed.

Henry and Charles both reached up simultaneously and pressed the power button on the headlamps attached to their EGO masks. Both lights came on and any area Henry and Charles looked out toward was now illuminated by a small, orange-tinged light protruding from their forehead.

Charles stepped in front of Henry and toward the mausoleum.

"Stay close and follow me. Keep that gun pointed down at all times, the last thing I need is my ass blown off," Charles explained.

"Got it, sir!" Henry confirmed as he adjusted the barrel toward the dirt.

Henry turned right and gave Ruby a final quick glance of humorous worry while shrugging his shoulders before he followed closely behind Charles to the mausoleum door.

Now standing at the face of the door, Charles grasped the padlock attached to the latch in his free hand. He pulled the lock toward himself to reveal the keyhole on the bottom. The door creaked and rattled as Charles adjusted the padlock in the light of his headlamp. He uncocked the hammer to his revolver and returned it to his waistband before he reached into his pants pocket and pulled out the key to the lock. Charles went to insert the key into the keyhole, but before he could, the mausoleum door shook violently, accompanied by a loud boom.

Charles, startled by the sudden eruption of the door, let go of the padlock and staggered backward toward the left side of the mausoleum, creating space between him and Henry. The door continued to rattle and shake against its hinges as it was forcefully beaten on from the other side.

"Oh fuck! It's in there! ... Henry, get back, ready your gun!" Charles ordered as he returned the key to his pocket.

Henry lifted the shotgun and aimed it at the door as he began to step backward. After he covered 10 meters of distance he turned around, ran back toward Ruby and positioned himself in front of her, shielding her from the danger.

"Stay behind me! I got you," Henry sternly told Ruby.

Ruby heard the authority and eloquence in Henry's muffled voice and thought it was comforting. She could see how much he cared and wanted to keep her safe. Ruby internally decided at this moment she would stop fighting herself on the fact she had feelings for him. Ruby got closer to Henry and rested her hand on his shoulder.

Charles retrieved his revolver, cocked the hammer back, and aimed at the door. He began to slowly step backward toward the left side of the mausoleum, keeping his aim firm.

The door shook ferociously with more and more force, slowly causing the wood to begin to crack and splinter. Eventually, with one final blow, the door broke open, and from within the darkness emerged a deer.

The deer charged past Charles as he followed its movement with his revolver. He had a clear shot but chose not to take it because he noticed Henry and Ruby were now positioned behind the deer, within his line of fire.

The deer turned and took charge toward Henry, kicking up patches of dirt, burrowing its head down to point its antlers at him.

"Kill it!" Charles yelled at the pair.

Henry racked the shotgun and aimed it at the deer.

"Henry, don't!" Ruby pleaded.

Henry halted his actions. He lowered the weapon and quickly glanced back at Ruby. Henry saw the worry in her face and decided he couldn't harm the deer. He turned back to the creature charging toward him and saw he needed to act fast. He turned around to face Ruby and, whilst gripping the shotgun with one hand, Henry swung both arms around her as he pushed their bodies out of harm's way.

The deer charged past, nearly missing the pair, whilst the deer's antler clipped and slid across Henry's back, slicing him from his left shoulder across to his right, leaving his work shirt torn and shredded behind the collar. Henry's back began to bleed and soak his shirt. He outstretched his arms in pain, dropping the gun and falling on Ruby as they both landed on the ground.

"Ahhhhhh!" Henry screamed out in pain as he fell.

"Henry, are you okay!?" Ruby asked, intensely worried, as she tried to frantically hold and comfort Henry as he lay halfway over top of her.

"Motherfucker! … Henry, you alright?" Charles asked as he ran over toward the pair, still staring at the deer.

"Fuck! … ah … No!" Henry said through his pain and gritted teeth as he tried to lift his torso off Ruby with his forearms.

Charles uncocked the hammer to his revolver and returned it to his waistband as he watched the deer flee and disappear into the darkened foliage. Charles then turned back toward the pair.

"Ruby, help me get him up and back to the truck. I got some medical supplies in Station 1 that will help," Charles commanded as he went to assist Henry.

Ruby carefully slid herself out from underneath Henry as he soaked in his pain. She picked up the shotgun off the ground, and began assisting Henry up from the grass. Charles and Ruby both stood on either side of Henry as each of them carefully gripped underneath his arms and lifted him up. Henry cascaded his upper body over Charles and Ruby's shoulders as they both aided him back to the truck.

12:31 AM

Henry sat shirtless in a chair within Station 1. As he laid his torso over Charles' desk, Ruby sat perpendicular to Henry and proceeded to use antiseptic and paper towels to clean his wound.

Ruby was awed by Henry and the state of his body silently as she thought about how he had saved her from getting hurt. Henry had inadvertently caused Ruby to become completely infatuated with him and had no idea of it.

Charles emerged from the back room of Station 1, holding a small syrette in his hand.

"Alright, Henry, don't ask how I got this, but it should make you feel right as rain," Charles explained.

"Right as what?" Henry asked, confused.

"Oh, that's that thing when the sky floods and drips, right?" Ruby interjected with a question.

"Shit, you kids never had a chance to really live. Anyway, this is pain medicine, really fucking strong pain medicine," Charles said.

Charles removed the plastic cap from the syrette and swiftly jabbed Henry in the shoulder. The needle pierced his skin and released the chemicals into his body. The pain of the wound began to subside, and Henry finally could relax his muscles. Charles removed the syrette from Henry's shoulder and threw it away in the trash.

"There ya go! Feel any better?" Charles asked Henry.

"Yeah, that helped," Henry said as he came down from the intense pain.

"Ruby, there's bandages and medical tape in the top left drawer of my desk; grab 'em and finish patching Henry up. When you're done, I'm taking you back to the Portway. Henry, I still need you," Charles informed the pair.

"For what?" Henry asked, confused.

Charles turned away from Henry and Ruby, staring out the Station windows deep into the forest.

Charles took in a powerful inhale before he sighed.

"The Epigone escaped ... it's still out there ... now, it's not leaving alive," Charles said ominously.

"You mean that deer? What's your plan now?" Henry asked in annoyed concern.

"Henry … the execution hour is upon us," Charles said with a stoic disposition.

7:35 AM

Henry trudged his feet along the street asphalt as he walked through the Homelands Dome. Henry felt fatigue flow through his body like blood. He could barely muster the energy to walk.

"Hello? Henry, are you there?" Ruby's voice came out of Henry's radio.

Unexpectedly hearing Ruby's voice come out of the radio made Henry slightly jump in his skin. Henry reached over, slowly unclipped the radio, and struggled to raise it to his mouth. Henry used his index finger to press the red button and began to speak.

"Yep … I'm here …" Henry said in a drained demeanor.

"What happened last night? Is everything okay? What did Charles mean by execution hour?" Ruby asked with repetitive concern.

"Uh, no … it's not okay. I, Uh, I kinda don't wanna talk about it …" Henry said, defeated, trying to avoid the subject.

"Henry, come over to my house. You don't sound good," Ruby requested.

"It's fine, I don't want to bother you. Plus, we should get some sleep anyway; we gotta work tonight," Henry said, trying not to be a burden.

"Henry, you better come over here right now, or I'm leaving and coming to get you," Ruby said with passionate care.

"Fine. ... I'll be there soon," Henry reluctantly accepted.

7:57 AM

Henry took a final step forward and was now standing in the center of Ruby's porch at the face of her front door. Henry retrieved his radio from his belt once again and radioed to Ruby.

"I'm here," Henry said.

Henry returned his radio to its spot on his belt and waited for Ruby to answer the door.

Henry stared down at his sneakers and saw dried blood splattered across the toe boxes. Henry then lifted his hands and began to inspect them. He noticed they were also covered in dry blood splatters and were stained a faded maroon. Henry stared at his hands for a moment as he saw horrific flashbacks of the work night he just endured.

Henry's traumatic visions were interrupted when he heard Ruby's front door open.

Henry looked up from his hands to catch sight of Ruby, but before he could adjust his vision, she had already lunged forward and wrapped her arms around his torso, giving him a gentle, tight hug. Henry felt Ruby's warmth flood around himself in her embrace. This loving act brought Henry's mind out of its dark pit and back to earth.

"Henry! I'm so happy you're okay! What happened!?!?" Ruby asked as she submerged her head into Henry's chest.

"He made me … kill them. He made me kill them all," Henry slowly let the words fall out of his mouth.

"What? Kill who?" Ruby asked.

"Charles made me execute every single deer in the park. All the deer that lived in Sanctuary are gone. He forced me to help him make a corpse pile behind the Crypt. That fat fuck goes and locks a deer in the Crypt and makes ME kill them all … fucking target practice, he says. He probably just made me kill for his dinner. I can still see all the blood and guts …" Henry said in dissociative annoyance that led into a scoffed rant.

"Oh no. … I'm so sorry, Henry," Ruby said as she proceeded to hug him tighter.

Ruby paused for a second, widely opening her eyes in surprise, as she was startled by a realization she had made within her train of thought.

"Henry? …" Ruby asked, with her head in his chest, in a slightly fearful tone.

"Yeah?" Henry asked in return.

"… Be honest with me. … Do you think we should tell anyone Charles has a gun? Doesn't it seem like he could be behind the disappearances?" Ruby pondered to Henry, worried about both their safety.

Henry was silent for a moment as his eyes darted around his thoughts, debating the answer to the question.

"Hmm ... I don't think so ... I mean, he could've killed me last night ... if he wanted to, why didn't he? ... and a Peace Officer was at Sanctuary yesterday. They probably questioned Charles; I mean, if you and I have been questioned, then he definitely was. Even if he was the murderer, why give me a gun to use? None of it is adding up," Henry answered, confused.

"Henry ... can I be honest with you?" Ruby asked, in a shy hesitation.

"Of course," Henry consoled.

"I think, for the first time in a long time, I'm actually getting a little worried. ... I don't want to be in a horror movie," Ruby said, trying to open up as the newfound weight of their small world was caving in.

"Don't worry. We'll both watch out for each other, remember? I won't give up on the pact. Plus, if Charles tries anything, I'll just blast em' with his own gun," Henry said, trying to be a courageous figure to soothe Ruby's worries.

"Thanks, Henry," Ruby said, uplifted, as she somewhat relaxed from her stress, knowing she wasn't alone.

Ruby hugged Henry tighter, squeezing him into a deeper, loving embrace.

Henry closed his eyes, let his head fall back slightly, sat in his skin, and just felt the sensation of being held in this moment.

Ruby pulled her head away from Henry's chest and looked up at his face. At this moment, Henry and Ruby were the closest face-to-face they had ever been. The gears in Ruby's head began turning. In the short time she had spent alone with Henry at this job, Ruby had developed a strong suspicion that he liked her, but she didn't pay any mind to it until she admitted to herself that she liked him back. Ruby thought to herself and decided she wanted to give Henry a gift for his efforts.

"Henry ..." Ruby said with a shy eagerness.

Henry opened his eyes, averted his attention away from his thoughts, and focused on Ruby.

"Wha-" Henry tried to ask before being interrupted.

Ruby took her arms away from surrounding Henry's torso. She reached up and grabbed a hold of both sides of his face. Ruby pulled Henry in close and passionately pressed her lips against his.

Ruby kissed Henry before he could realize what was happening. Henry was stunned at first, but understanding that he was now experiencing the greatest moment of his life, he fed further into the kiss.The pair slowly melted into each other as they passionately continued to swap saliva. Ruby had saved Henry's sanity and made him feel cared for.

The momentum of the kiss naturally faded and the couple would pull away slowly to look each other in the eyes.

"Ya, know ... my parents won't be home till 5 ..." Ruby said with devious implications.

Henry smiled and Ruby pulled him by his work shirt collar as they both stepped inside her house. Henry wouldn't exit Ruby's home until several hours later.

Chapter 8

The Last Testament

January 22nd, 1994
9:34 PM
773 citizens remain

Henry arrived at the Homelands Portway door to find Ruby waiting for him.

Ruby wore the headphones to her cassette player over her ears and had her duffel bag strapped to her back. She kept her eyes closed as she danced by herself in front of the Portway door.

"Hey babe, having fun?" Henry asked.

Ruby couldn't hear Henry through the music she was listening to.

"Ruby!" Henry shouted.

Ruby finally heard Henry's muffled voice calling out to her and ceased dancing. She opened her eyes and looked over at him.

"Oh, hey, babe!" Ruby said, happy to see Henry, as she removed her headphones and hung them around her neck.

Ruby reached down and pressed the stop button on her cassette player before hitting the rewind button to reset the song at its beginning for future playback.

"What were you listening to?" Henry asked.

"My favorite song. Kinda reminds me of you," Ruby said.

"Oh really? Can I hear?" Henry asked.

"In due time," Ruby said.

"Can't wait. ... What's with the duffel bag?" Henry asked.

"Oh, I have a surprise for you!" Ruby said, excited.

"A surprise for me? Why?" Henry asked.

"Well, I just felt bad that you got hurt. I mean, you did kinda save my life," Ruby explained.

"What? Yeah right! I wouldn't go that far," Henry said, downplaying his importance.

"Oh, C'mon Henry. I saw your back. That deer could've seriously hurt me," Ruby said, stressing Henry's importance.

"Well, either way. You didn't have to get me anything; you've already done so much," Henry said with appreciative satisfaction, alluding to certain things.

"Maybe so, but I wanted to," Ruby said with a smile.

Henry was happy to see Ruby cared for him as much as he desperately wanted for his whole life.

Ruby stepped forward and pressed the Call Kart button.

10:06 PM

Henry and Ruby began to walk through Sanctuary, conversing.

"So ... what's this surprise?" Henry asked, intrigued.

"More like where," Ruby said.

"Where? What do you mean?" Henry asked.

Before Ruby could further explain Charles came over both radios.

"Henry and Ruby, are you guys here yet? Over," Charles asked.

Henry unclipped and retrieved his radio from his belt.

"Yes, sir. Me and Ruby just got into the Dome. Over," Henry said.

"Good to hear. Henry, tonight it's your turn to change the ARS filter. Try to do it as soon as possible. Over," Charles said.

"Got it, sir. Over," Henry said.

Henry returned his radio to his belt.

"Hey, what a coincidence?" Ruby rhetorically asked.

"What is?" Henry asked in return.

"That's where the surprise is," Ruby explained.

"It's at the ARS?" Henry asked.

"Patience is a virtue … you'll see; let's go grab a filter from Station 2," Ruby said

10:28 PM

The couple walked across Sanctuary Park until they arrived at Station 2. Once there, Henry procured the shotgun, loaded it with five shells, strapped the gun to his back, and grabbed an ARS filter from the Station. Henry and Ruby then left Station 2 and began to walk toward the ARS.

10:47 PM

When the couple arrived on the opposite end of the Dome, the ARS and Station 3 were off in the horizon, obscured by the trees. The pair continued their journey until Ruby had stopped walking and gazed amongst her surroundings in the forest. She had finally chosen a spot.

Henry turned around and stared at Ruby, confused.

"Are you ready for the surprise? Ruby asked.

"Ready as I'll ever be, I guess," Henry said.

Ruby bent down and took off her duffel bag, placing it on the grass beneath her. She unzipped the biggest pocket on the bag and began pulling out an assortment of different items.

"What's all this?" Henry asked.

"I made us a picnic," Ruby said happily.

"Really?" Henry asked, surprised.

"You bet. My brave little executioner deserves a nice meal," Ruby said jokingly.

Henry laughed at Ruby's comment as it brought hilarity to his dark reality.

Once Ruby had pulled everything she needed out of her bag, she began to set up the picnic. She laid out a blanket, set out two bottles of *Green Genie*, laid out two paper plates, and pulled out cold pizza wrapped in aluminum foiling. She positioned everything on top of the blanket to be in its proper spot and sat down. Henry walked over to the blanket, set the ARS filter out in the grass, and sat down in the spot laid out for him.

Ruby tore open the aluminum foil and distributed a slice of pizza between the plates.

The couple then began to eat.

"Henry?" Ruby asked as she chewed and swallowed.

"Yeah?" Henry asked in response as he also chewed and consumed his bite.

"What do you want out of life?" Ruby asked.

"Wow, we're getting deep, huh?" Henry chuckled as he asked.

"I'm just genuinely curious. What makes you tick?" Ruby asked.

Henry thought for a moment.

"I don't know, I don't wanna die next, that's for sure. I uh, I guess ... hmm, I guess I just want happiness," Henry said.

"What does that entail for you?" Ruby asked.

"Hmmm ... At this point, probably just being with the people I love for as long as I can. ... How about you?" Henry answered.

"I want to live life to the fullest. I mean, I don't want to die either, but what I really want is to stop holding myself back and just take more leaps, ya know? Just drop all the bullshit ... but it's difficult," Ruby explained.

"Why should it be so difficult?" Henry asked.

"What do you mean?" Ruby asked in return.

"I mean, with all that's going on. Why not do everything you can do while you can? If we're all trapped under these Dome walls, never to leave, people are disappearing, and nothing is ever going to get better, then why not live like there's no tomorrow? We don't even know if there will be a tomorrow. Why don't you and I start living for once? From now on, we should do the most we can with our lives," Henry explained emphatically.

Ruby heard what Henry said and became convinced.

"Y-yeah … Yes! Sounds like a plan!" Ruby agreed.

Henry picked up the unopened bottle of *Green Genie* that sat in front of him and lifted it to make a toast with Ruby.

"To finally living!" Henry said.

"To finally living!" Ruby said as she lifted her unopened bottle of *Green Genie*.

The couple clinked the glass bottles together and both untwisted their caps simultaneously.

Henry lifted his bottle to his lips and drank a big gulp of the beverage. Ruby went to lift her bottle but stopped as she read her fortune.

"*In haste, express thine truest heart. For I fear, there is no tomorrow,*" was printed on the cap.

Ruby, reading the fortune and thinking of what she and Henry had just toasted to, got the feeling that this was her moment to prove herself.

Ruby's feelings for Henry had developed from a strange friendship, out of loneliness and proximity, into something much more. The numerous growing implications of unforeseen death from daily life in Cherry Blossom accelerated her emotions and convinced her that available time was inevitably becoming scarce. Ruby had decided that she couldn't deny her heart; she knew there was an unspoken special connection between her and Henry. He meant more to her than she could've originally predicted.

Ruby had faith in her fortune; she believed that if she didn't take action in this moment, it would be the antithesis of what she feared and the opportunity would flee from her, only for her to chase after it again. She felt that if she really wanted to go after her happiness and live up to what she now set out to do with her life, she needed to let go of the nervous worries that held her back and tell Henry how she actually felt.

Ruby felt her heart intensely beating inside her chest. She could hardly catch her breath. Ruby paused before pulling the metaphorical trigger.

"Henry … I want to tell you something before it's too late …" Ruby stated nervously.

Henry lowered the bottle of *Green Genie* and lifted his opposite hand to read his fortune. He kept his eyesight locked onto the bottle cap as he was half paying attention to Ruby.

"What's up?" Henry playfully asked, not fully understanding the seriousness of the situation.

Henry read his fortune internally to himself.

"*The Martyr must choose: Life or Love?*" was printed on the cap.

Once Henry read the printed inscription, he was confused. Before he could further ponder on the fortune, Ruby gently put her hand over the bottle cap and lowered his hand out of sight. Ruby commanded Henry's attention in a tender assertiveness.

Henry's pupils ascended to meet Ruby's. The couple locked eyes.

"Henry ... I know we've only really spoken for a month, but ... it feels different with you, ya know? I get it; this is gonna sound weird, *but* ... since time to live it up may be running out and you really want to spend your time with the ones you love, then ... I love you, Henry, what do you say?" Ruby propositioned as she blushed and smiled deviously.

Henry sat in stunned silence until his eyes fluttered back to reality and he quickly confessed his truth.

"I love you too, Ruby," Henry said.

Henry had now sealed his fate.

Ruby, hearing Henry's response, set her bottle down and quickly stood up from the ground as her eyes began to weep with joy. Henry saw this and set his bottle down to slowly rise to his feet.

Both now stood in front of each other at either end of the blanket. Henry and Ruby walked around and met at one side of the blanket so as not to disturb the picnic. Ruby closed her eyes and wrapped her arms around Henry tighter than ever before. Henry held Ruby with the same amount of passion. The idea of the fortune quickly faded away and Henry now only cared about how he achieved, quite possibly, his biggest dream.

After a long embrace, the couple separated and Ruby opened her eyes to see a flashing yellow light behind Henry, emitting from the ARS.

"Oh, shit," Ruby said as she pointed toward the light.

Henry twisted his body to see what had alerted Ruby. When he noticed the ARS was pulsating yellow, Henry slowly let go of her.

"Fuck, we gotta go change the filter," Henry said as he stared out toward the light that beckoned him.

Henry bent over and grasped the handle of the ARS filter tightly in his hand. He lifted the filter, turned back to Ruby and stuck his free hand out toward her.

"Time to live," Henry said as an offering of opportunity toward Ruby.

Ruby smiled at Henry before placing her hand on his. The couple interlocked their fingers and held onto one another as they left the picnic behind, traversing toward the light.

11:03 PM

Henry and Ruby stared at the ARS. They couldn't believe what they saw.

The ARS filter within the machine had been freshly punctured and severely damaged, draining its purple contents down the face of the device. The cause of the puncture was a broken-off deer antler protruding from the wound in the filter.

Henry stared at the antler, pondering its very existence; he couldn't make any sense of the sight before him.

"Wow, that's pretty strange," Ruby said.

"Yeah ... it is ... " Henry said, deeply confused.

"What's the matter?" Ruby asked.

"I know we killed every deer in the park. How did this happen?" Henry asked

"Maybe it happened before then and it only started failing now?" Ruby suggested.

"Yeah ... maybe ... " Henry, feeling uneasy, tried to agree.

Henry removed the empty filter from the ARS. He lifted the new filter and shoved it into the empty slot in the machine. The lights atop the ARS had now returned to their solid green state.

Henry lifted and inspected the broken filter. Ruby walked over to Henry and slowly took the filter from his hands, taking his mind away from it. She threw the filter on the ground and stared deep into his eyes. Henry quickly forgot about the filter and felt mesmerized.

Ruby removed the cassette player from her belt. She unplugged the headphones and spun the volume dial till it was at its maximum.

Ruby took the cassette player, slid her free hand halfway into Henry's pants, pulled him in closer and clipped it onto his belt. She pressed the play button on the device and stepped backward as she took Henry by the hand.

A happy-sounding despondent song, drenched in hopeless undertones, began to play from the speaker of the cassette player as Ruby led Henry away from the ARS.

Once they were a short distance from the ARS, Ruby began to dance out in the forest. Henry joined in with her and the couple began to giggle as they danced poorly together to the music in the air.

Henry and Ruby swam in the dopamine that flooded their brains.

They had found the happiness both so desperately sought in each other.

The mood quickly decayed and Ruby slowly ceased dancing at the sight of something inexplicable.

"What? what's the matter?" Henry asked, confused, when he saw Ruby's face had deformed from happy to worried.

"Who … who is that?" Ruby asked as she pointed out into the shadows.

Henry turned around and saw someone out in the darkness of the forest walking toward them. Once the individual stepped out into the moonlight, Henry could see who it was. He reached over to the cassette player on his belt and hit pause.

There was a moment of silence before Henry called out to her.

"Gwen? … " Henry asked, bewildered.

"Help me … " Gwen said through tears, visibly distraught.

Gwendolyn Moore, 21 years old, had shoulder-length platinum blonde hair, a nose ring, and was an avid graffiti artist. She currently appeared mangled and maltreated. Her skin was pale and stained with random splotches of blood. She still wore her Filter Factory uniform from the day she vanished. Her left ear was severed off and missing, leaving a bloody opening in the side of her head that leaked heavily down her face.

Ruby stepped in front of Henry and walked over toward Gwen.

Henry was now pontificating about how strange this was. He couldn't believe they had found a missing citizen. Henry started to become worried and felt a sense of danger permeate around him. He began to glance around the forest in search of a cause for this feeling within.

"Gwen, are you okay? Where have you been? Who hurt you?" Ruby asked as she got closer to her.

Henry continued to think about how strange this current situation was. He searched out further in the forest for an answer before he glanced back toward the ARS. He focused his eyesight on the filter lying out in the grass. The antler protruding from the broken filter was no longer there and was now replaced with a severed human ear lying on the ground next to the metal casing.

Henry quickly turned to look back at Ruby.

"Ruby, wait!!!" Henry shouted as he finally came to a horrific realization.

Henry was too late; Ruby had gotten too close to Gwen.

When Ruby turned away from her, leaving herself vulnerable, Gwen began to twitch and convulse. The sound of bones cracking and shifting emitted from within her body.

Suddenly, Gwen began to not resemble herself anymore. Her pupils had faded and her eyes began to glow a baby blue. Her skin was turning gray, seemingly congealing and reforming itself into a grotesque abomination. Two thin, long arms grew from her back. Her face had elongated and morphed, representing that of a disfigured deer. The torso of the creature grew taller and became gaunt. Its legs had bent backward and stretched longways, increasing its height to roughly two-and-a-half meters tall. Within an instant, the facade of Gwendolyn Moore had melted away and left entirely.

Henry felt trepidation within his soul.

Charles was right; the Epigone was real.

Ruby turned and watched as the imitation of Gwen transformed right in front of her. She was frozen in fear, unable to conceive what her eyes were seeing.

The Epigone reached forward and picked Ruby up off the ground.

"Henry!!!" Ruby screamed in a high-pitched shriek.

Henry snapped out of his terror and quickly retrieved the shotgun from his back. He racked the forestock and put a shell into the chamber. Henry lifted the gun and aimed it at the Epigone. He couldn't get a clear shot without hitting Ruby.

The Epigone lifted Ruby closer to its face. The creature's deer mouth opened and split into three separate parts, each aligned with a row of sharp, jagged teeth. The Epigone wrapped its mouth around Ruby's forearm and took a bite out of her, removing a sizable chunk of flesh.

"Aaaaaaaaaaaahhhhhhhh!!!!" Ruby screamed in agony.

Henry witnessed this happen and quickly pointed the gun at the Epigone's legs. He pulled the trigger and a slug was fired from the barrel. The projectile hit the Epigone, ripping through its skin and bone, severing its leg in half.

The Epigone toppled over and was ripped to the ground by gravity, releasing Ruby from its grasp and dropping her violently in the process.

The Epigone now turned its attention on Henry. It bent backward as its skin amalgamated and rejoined with its separations, reattaching itself to its leg once again. The creature then began to slink and slither in a prone plod across the grass toward him before commencing to sprint.

Henry staggered back before he ran toward the ARS and the Epigone chased him down, swallowing the distance, until it was right behind him. Henry turned to face inevitable doom and was now trapped with his back pressed up against the machine.

The Epigone lurked over Henry and slowly lifted an arm up. Henry saw as jagged, broken bones emerged and surfaced out of its palm, forming a sharp makeshift stinger. The Epigone reached back before driving its newly formed stinger-hand into Henry's right shoulder, skewering through his body and into the machine, pinning him against the ARS.

"Fuuuuuuuuck!!!" Henry screamed in pain.

Henry started to panic. He quickly looked at his surroundings. Henry began to go into shock before he caught a glimpse of Ruby's body lying out in the grass. He knew he needed to save her.

In that moment Henry's adrenaline took an overwhelming hold on him. Henry gripped the forestock of the shotgun tight before shoving the backstock against the ARS and, whilst using one hand, racked the forestock, sending a new shell into the chamber. Using the same hand, he positioned the shotgun's grip into his right hand and slid his finger onto the trigger.

As Henry did this action the Epigone crept its body forward and opened the parts of its mouth to try and consume his face.

Henry fired another slug into the Epigone's torso.

The Epigone's chest exploded, covering Henry's hands and arms in its blood. The creature recoiled back and retracted its arm from Henry's shoulder. The abomination began to violently twitch, erratically flailing its limbs, trying to attack as it drowned in pain.

Henry fell to the ground and quickly staggered to his feet, running over toward Ruby.

The Epigone lunged forward and began to destroy the ARS.

Henry reached Ruby's body and knelt down next to her.

"Ruby, C'mon, get up; we gotta go!" Henry shouted as he shook her.

Ruby didn't respond. She was knocked unconscious from the fall and still losing a profuse amount of blood.

Henry didn't waste any time. He quickly swung the shotgun strap over his head and let the gun rest across his back. Henry slid his arms under Ruby's shoulders and legs. Fueled by determination, he lifted her with ease.

When Henry stood up, holding Ruby firm in his grasp, he heard an uncanny sound starting to broadcast from the ARS.

As Henry turned around and looked back, he now saw the ARS flashing red and sounding the Dome Meltdown Alarm siren.

There was a pause as Henry witnessed that the ARS was so badly damaged it was now engulfed in flames and Ultra-18 was spewing out through the holes created in the machine.

As the Epigone stretched its arm back for a final devastating attack Henry was stunned in place.

"Oh fuck ... " Henry said, in anticipation of what he suspected was about to happen.

The Epigone swung forward and punctured through the heart of the ARS, causing the machine to malfunction and break entirely. The ARS exploded, flooding a huge billowing cloud of Ultra-18 into the Sanctuary Dome. Henry turned and sprinted as fast as he could toward the Portway door, holding Ruby close.

The cloud of Ultra-18 quickly surrounded and engulfed Henry and Ruby.

Henry was inhaling excess amounts of the gas due to his rapid breathing. The cloud was thick and hard to see through. Henry began to cough and wheeze, dropping Ruby on the ground as he fell to his knees. Henry convulsed on the grass as the gas blinded and choked him. He reached forward and held onto Ruby's leg as he thrashed around for air before eventually being able to breathe within the gas, succumbing to the side effects of Ultra-18.

Henry drowned further in panic as he was struggling to see around inside the gas cloud. As Henry tried to evaluate his escape, he heard a noise that plagued him with dread.

From behind Henry, inside the cloud of Ultra-18 that surrounded him, he could hear the Epigone growl toward him. Henry slowly turned to face the sound. All he could see was gas and darkness.

Henry turned back and began to feel around Ruby's body so he could lift her again. As he slid his hand around her waist, he felt the emergency flare inside Ruby's utility belt brush against his finger. Henry quickly slid it out of its pouch and held the red tube in his hand.

The Epigone growled at him once again and he could tell it was closer than before.

Henry removed the plastic cap off the flare and placed the top of it against the ignitor. He torqued the flare against the cap and ignited a bright red flame that illuminated a small perimeter around him in a scarlet haze.

Henry turned around and could see the Epigone's bright baby blue eyes piercing through the gas, staring straight at him. The Epigone stood a meter away from Henry, only separated by Ultra-18. The creature slowly crept toward him until it was half a meter away, within arm's reach.

Henry looked down at Ruby's body and took note of her position in the gas. He then faced the Epigone a final time.

The sight of the flame in Henry's hand gave him an idea. He quickly decided he was going to drive the burning flame into the abomination's face.

Henry reached back before he lunged forward and seared the lit flare into the Epigone's right eye, causing the creature to shriek and cower in pain, disappearing back into the cloud.

Henry, using one hand, gripped and lifted Ruby's torso up by her work shirt and slid his arm under both of hers, across her chest. Henry stood up with Ruby lifelessly hanging over his arm and pointed the flare into the gas toward the Epigone. He held Ruby close to his chest as he took steps backward and dragged her along the grass, creating distance between the pair and the monster.

Henry was beginning to hallucinate as further side effects from being exposed. The colors of everything surrounding him were slowly becoming vibrant and neon.

Henry finally lowered his arm and dropped the flare to the ground. He reached down and swung his arm under Ruby's legs and lifted her up across his chest. Henry turned back and ran with Ruby in his grasp until he finally exited the cloud of Ultra-18 and could see the surrounding area clearly.

Still having a slight grasp on reality, Henry could see off in the distance the headlights of Charles' truck heading toward him. Henry ran toward the truck but halted his movement halfway when he saw the truck was traveling at a lethal speed directly at him. Henry stood in the grass, waiting to see if he needed to leap out of the way to save both Ruby and himself.

Once Charles was a short distance from Henry, he slammed on the brakes and the inertia caused the truck to drift in the dirt, stopping a meter in front of him. The headlights shined upon Henry and revealed a petrified soul standing out in the grass, holding a body in his hands.

Charles put the truck in park, exited the vehicle and left it running. He retrieved his revolver from his waistband and aimed it directly at Henry.

"Is that really you?" Charles asked in curious suspicion.

"Yes! Yes, it's me!" Henry answered in fear.

"What's your last name?" Charles sternly asked.

"What?" Henry asked, confused by the question.

Charles cocked the hammer to his revolver.

"It's Greene. My last name is Greene!" Henry quickly answered in fear of getting shot.

Charles quickly deflated from his hostility and slightly lowered his weapon. He stared at Henry with a stern look.

"Load her in, I'll cover you. Once we get moving, I'll give you a rag; tie it tightly 'round that arm above the wound," Charles said as he aimed his revolver at the large cloud of Ultra-18 creeping toward them.

Henry ran to the back side of the vehicle, opened the tailgate, and laid Ruby down in the bed of the truck. He slid her body forward and proceeded to climb into the truck bed with her. Henry reached back and closed the tailgate before he bent down to check on Ruby. Charles ran back and got into the driver's seat of the truck. He reached into the glove compartment and pulled out an old handkerchief. Charles opened the back window of the truck and handed Henry the rag. Henry tied the rag tightly around Ruby's arm and tried to wake her but was unsuccessful.

"I already called the Kart and opened both doors. When we get there, you get her in that Kart!" Charles instructed from inside the truck.

"Understood!" Henry said.

Charles put the truck into gear and drove in a tight semicircle to face the Portway door before he pressed with full force on the gas pedal, traveling as fast as he could along the serpentined path toward the exit.

Henry turned and gazed through the separations in the trees toward the back of the Sanctuary Dome as they got closer to the Portway door. He could see the cloud of Ultra-18 had now enveloped almost one-third of the Dome.

Henry stared deep into the misty horizon for the Epigone, searching frantically for any sign of the creature. After a short moment, Henry saw the monster's silhouette emerge out of the gas cloud and canter straight toward them.

"Charles! It's coming back!" Henry shouted.

The Epigone sprinted at an incredible speed with rage and determination. The distance between all was consumed in just a few short moments and the abomination was now right behind the vehicle.

The trio was 40 meters away from the Sanctuary gate archway when the Epigone swung its arm, striking the truck underneath the tailgate, lifting it off the ground, and throwing Henry and Ruby out into Sanctuary. The truck rolled over in the air before ultimately crash-landing upside down on the ground, crushing the roof to the cabin inward, and trapping Charles inside. Henry and Ruby landed on the grass and dirt with audible thuds, causing Henry to now be struck unconscious.

Charles lay against the bent metal hood inside the wrecked truck, still conscious but slipping fast. He quickly searched around for the Epigone through the smashed glass and crushed openings in the vehicle as he could feel he was losing himself. Charles peered out the jagged metal of the driver-side window and saw the Epigone creeping toward the trio. Charles then submitted to the trauma done to his body and blacked out.

Henry, Ruby, and Charles were all now unconscious and unable to move. The trio lay spread apart as the Portway door was open and the Kart was ready to leave just mere meters away.

Chapter 9

The Crescendo

January 23rd, 1994
12:53 AM
772 citizens remain

Henry slowly came to. He opened his eyes and realized he was still in a deep hallucination.

Henry lifted his head and studied his surroundings as he lay on his side in the same position the inertia from the crash had left him. He saw everything around him was growing and shrinking in size. The grass was now a shallow sea of a milky sludge that rippled as Henry moved within it. The tree trunks were breathing heavily and the branches were now replaced with multi-tongued serpents that moved in slow motion. The leaves of the trees had become hands that reached out and grasped for the sky. The color of everything around him was a vibrant, pastel, iridescent version of itself. As he observed the visions his eyes cast to his brain, Henry tried to obtain a grip on his new reality.

Henry looked ahead and could see Ruby lying unconscious a short distance in front of him. He glanced backward over his shoulder and saw three-quarters of the Sanctuary Dome was now full of Ultra-18 and the cloud of gas was slowly getting closer to the truck containing Charles. The vehicle was partially engulfed in a small inferno, actively growing and consuming the engine block.

Henry could still tell through his malformed eyesight that Charles was in the remains of the truck and Ruby was lying closer to the Portway door. He currently was equidistant between them.

Henry struggled to rise to his feet. Once he was standing, he began to limp toward Ruby, grunting in pain with every step.

As he got closer to her, Henry lifted his hand and felt the blood leaking down his face from his tear ducts. He pulled his hand away and stared at the coating on his fingers and palm, taking in the sight as a sign of the trouble he was in.

Henry recognized the blood was secreting from his eyes and he was currently experiencing stage 3 of Ultra-18 poisoning known as "the Blood Tears." His pupils rose up from the sight of blood glistening off his hand before him. He focused on the image of Ruby lying motionless ahead and dropped his hand to his side before continuing forward.

As Charles slowly awoke, he could hear the grunts of pain Henry emitted as he staggered away. Charles inspected the current situation he was in and, using all of his available energy, shimmied his body around the inside of the truck until he could press his face up against the opening of the partially flattened passenger window. He searched around for the Epigone but could only see Henry and Ruby out of the narrow opening.

"Henry … " Charles painfully grunted.

Henry halted in place and slowly oscillated his vision over at Charles.

"Henry … you gotta help me … I can't get myself out," Charles pleaded.

Henry glanced forward and observed Ruby's body for a moment before he turned back again to Charles. He then stared up at the cloud of Ultra-18 as it was rolling in and knew he only had enough time to save one of them.

He had to make a decision.

This was Henry's ultimatum, a choice between life or love.

Henry thought for a moment before he chose what must be done.

He turned away from Charles and faced Ruby a final time before stepping closer to her.

"Henry, no ... please don't do this ... it's going to come back ... " Charles pleaded more.

Henry felt horrible for the act he was committing and began to tear up slightly.

"I'm sorry, Charles. ... I need to save her ..." Henry said as he struggled further to walk over toward Ruby.

Henry chose to let Charles die to save his love.

Once he made it over to her body, Henry bent down and slid his arms under Ruby. He commanded his body to push through its pain and misery, slowly lifting her up off the ground. Henry suffered through the wounds that corroded him to hold her close in a loving grasp as he began to escort her to the Portway door.

"Henry! Please! Don't leave me!" Charles pleaded once more.

Henry marched faster toward the open Portway door as he heard Charles beg for his life.

Charles gazed on at Henry trotting away past the Sanctuary gate, in the midst of abandoning him, and noticed something odd about Ruby's arm flailing at Henry's side. Charles recognized that the bite taken out of Ruby's arm before was now missing, with fresh skin in its place. Charles searched out on the ground where Ruby was lying before Henry picked her up and saw painted on the grass in the flickering clarity of light from the truck's inferno was a thick pool of blood, much more than Ruby's wound could produce. Charles quickly glanced over toward Henry as he realized what had actually occurred.

"Henry! No! Wait!!!!" Charles screamed the loudest he could for a final time.

It was too late. Henry had already stepped inside the Portway Kart and was out of earshot of Charles.

Henry walked over to the cushioned seats that hugged the outer walls of the Kart and laid Ruby's body down on top. Once Henry let go of her, he turned around to face the control panel.

Henry, still seeing hallucinations, lightly felt around the control panel made up of eyeballs and a misshapen shovel until he found the emergency button. Henry hesitated before submerging his finger into the blood-filled eyeball within the panel. Once activated Henry turned and witnessed as both the Portway door and Portway Kart door shut rapidly, accompanied by louder metallic booms.

When Charles saw the Portway door close, he frantically tried, through agonizing pain and broken bones, to retrieve his radio from his belt.

114

The lights inside the Portway Kart turned red and pulsated as the Kart quickly moved along its tracks.

Henry ran back toward the Portway Kart door and stared out the window nestled within it. He witnessed as the Sanctuary Portway door got smaller in the distance.

Henry observed as he was now leaving Sanctuary behind.

Henry removed the shotgun from his back and pressed his blood-soaked hand against the glass, leaving a maroon handprint that dripped down the pane. He hung his head in sorrow. Henry felt horrible about what he did to Charles, but he knew it was the only way to save Ruby. He turned around, pressed his back into the Portway Kart door, slid down, and fell to the floor. Henry rested against the Kart door and laid the shotgun across his lap. He closed his eyes and soaked in his trauma.

"Please remain calm. Emergency personnel and Peace Officers will be awaiting you in the Central Hub," a female voice recording announced from the speaker within the control panel.

Henry thought the horror was now over … it had only just begun.

"Henry, that's not Ruby!!!" Charles' distorted voice shouted out of Henry's radio.

Henry opened his eyes, widened with fear, and immediately stared at Ruby's body.

Ruby's eyes opened and Henry saw that they were glowing baby blue.

The Epigone, disguised as Ruby, sat up on the cushioned seats, swung its legs over the edge, and rose to its feet. The creature stepped forward and stood in the center of the Kart, staring Henry down. The horrid anomaly convulsed and shook as its mouth split open into three sections, each aligned with sharp teeth. Four long, skinny stinger arms slowly emerged and grew out of its back, all pointing toward Henry.

Henry stared at the terrifying abomination preying upon him, knowing survival was most likely unfeasible. At this moment, with nothing left to lose except his life, Henry decided to endure the obstacle that stood before him on his own terms. He reached over to Ruby's cassette player, still clipped on his belt, and hit play.

Ruby's favorite song resumed playing and was a happy, vindictive contrast to the horrific reality that currently plagued Henry. He could still see the Epigone's imitation of his love staring back, wanting to consume him.

As the song played and the emergency lights drowned the foes in a vibrant rubellite, it created a morbid melancholic eeriness inside the Kart.

Henry gripped the shotgun tight and aimed the barrel at the Epigone with intentions to kill. He racked the forestock, sending a shell into the chamber, and stared at what awaited him with determination. Henry then began to slowly chuckle to himself before it grew to a deep, anguished laughter accompanied by a big smile plastered on his face.

Two entered the Portway, only for one to escape.

The End.

www.ingramcontent.com/pod-product-compliance
Lightning Source LLC
Chambersburg PA
CBHW070630130626
46555CB00006B/2506